Abo

My name is Tiare Fenrich and I am a thirty-six-year-old who grew up on a farm in a small town called Wilkie in Saskatchewan, Canada. I have ancestry in Fiji, New Zealand, Ireland and Germany. I lived in New Zealand for eight years, getting my degree in occupational therapy and specializing in mental health. While I was there my brother passed away at the age of nineteen due to an accidental overdose. He suffered from schizophrenia and had a huge impact on my life. I have always had a passion for writing since I was a kid, writing twelve journals throughout my life as well as poetry. I am a self-proclaimed artist, love snowboarding, fishing, exploring, sports and my dog, Tobi. I got inspired to write this book when I found some ghost flowers in Nelson, BC. I hope you enjoy the adventure as much as I did.

ALEX AND LANK'S GHOST FLOWER ADVENTURE

Tiare Aubryn Fenrich

ALEX AND LANK'S GHOST FLOWER ADVENTURE

Vanguard Press

VANGUARD PAPERBACK

A CIP catalogue record for this title is
available from the British Library.

ISBN 978-1-80016-027-9

Vanguard Press is an imprint of
Pegasus Elliot MacKenzie Publishers Ltd.
www.pegasuspublishers.com

First Published in 2021

Vanguard Press
Sheraton House Castle Park
Cambridge England

Printed & Bound in Great Britain

Dedication

I would like to dedicate this book to my dad, Marvin Fenrich. Thanks for taking so many chances in life, and on me. This book is also dedicated to my late brother, Marc Fenrich, for teaching me so many valuable lessons through his life and death.

Acknowledgements

Firstly, I would like to acknowledge and thank Plains Cree Elder, Herbalist and Ceremonial Leader; Barry L. Ahenakew from Ahtahkakoop Reserve; Starblanket, for giving his blessings on this book. I have so much respect for your culture, traditions, legends and ancestors. May you continue to guide us. In the same breath, I need to acknowledge my Creator for inspiring this story. There is no way I could have come up with this on my own.

To my mom and best friend, Deirdre Fenrich, thank you for your guidance and creative inspiration in my life, you mean the absolute world to me. I also would like to thank my sisters, Ruve and Lolomai Fenrich, for standing beside me through all of the ups and downs. I know it hasn't always been easy.

I would like to acknowledge Eloise Johnson, my high school English teacher, for pointing me in the right direction and having such an enthusiastic attitude towards this book. Your enthusiasm helped me continue to work towards making this dream become a reality.

My sincere gratitude to Helena Long from Phippen, Saskatchewan, for her editorial support. I am very fortunate to have met you and look forward to collaborating with you in the future. I am also very grateful for Kathy Heilman, my next door neighbour growing up, from Wilkie, Saskatchewan, who helped connect me to Helena and to the local paper. Thank-you both!

To my dear friend, Danya Kaminer, I am very grateful you have always been there for me and continue to cheer me on. You truly are a gem and I don't know what I would do without you.

Lastly, I would like to thank Brett Chasse from North Battleford, Saskatchewan, for being my rock through an extremely difficult time in my life; not to mention a pandemic. Your positive attitude and great sense of humor carried me through, more than you will ever know. I am grateful you supported me to launch this book and for giving me the idea to create an art studio; as much as I'm sure you regret that now.

It is through the unique sound of each note; carefully crafted together, working in collaboration with one another, that a magical song is born.

CHAPTER 1

On a serene and peaceful evening in the middle of July, the air was filled with warmth and comfort, as the stars began to show their light. Alex snuck out of the house quietly and tip-toed her way to the trampoline, scanning the scene to make sure the coast was clear. As she pulled herself up and flopped onto her back, she admired the stars in a complete state of contentment. Alone in silence, she felt as though the sky could swallow her whole. Every star fascinated her and she wondered about what existed on each one. She pondered whether there was life on other planets. That thought made her so excited. In science class she had learned that organisms could grow in extreme heat and extreme cold, so she figured life could easily grow on other planets.

In the midst of her personal reflection, she suddenly heard a rustling in the trees. Surprised, she quickly looked over to see what was there. As she peered over she saw a very tall figure outlined behind the bush. Looking closer, she could see really long straight blonde hair cascading from a tall looking creature. Extremely startled, she jolted up and bounced off the trampoline to sprint to the house. In her frenzy, she tripped on a tree stump and fell over.

'Oh my God,' she thought, 'I've broken my ankle.' Alex lay there in utter pain as she began to cry. As she attempted to drag herself up, she felt a hand on her shoulder and found herself locking eyes with a tall lanky figure. Completely speechless, she felt frozen with fear. Nothing could exit her mouth, not even a scream. In spite of this fear, she felt a sense of peace come over her; as if an energy of calm radiated her entire existence. As the creature looked at her with large peaceful black and yellow piercing eyes, she somehow ceased to feel afraid. She continued to stare in disbelief when the creature reached out its hand with extraordinarily long, skinny, twig like fingers and placed them on her ankle. As its fingers touched her ankle, she felt a hot tingling sensation, like all the rays of sunlight being targeted together at once. As the creature removed its hand, Alex no longer felt any pain. In fact, she could move her ankle around with ease.

"Th-th-thank you," she sputtered.

The creature gave a slow nod and was smiling through its eyes. As it backed away slowly, Alex could get a better look. Was it a human? She wasn't sure. She decided to call him Lank since he was so tall and lanky. No clothing, only long blonde hair and human-like body parts. Alex could not ignore her intense curiosity. What was Lank? Was it a man or a woman? Where did he come from? Alex had a very strong feeling that Lank was not a human. As she watched him walk away, she made a mental note that she would most definitely be following not far behind in the distance.

CHAPTER 2

Alex was somewhat of a tomboy who grew up in Nelson, British Colombia. She had curly long red hair and bright blue eyes. She had freckles all over her body and face. Her mom told her they were beauty marks; so she figured she must be *really* beautiful with all the freckles she had. She was ten years old and didn't have a best friend. At school she was acquaintances with everyone, yet not close friends with anyone. Everyone bugged her at the beginning of grade four and told her she was stupid. Her grades were failing and she had no idea how she would ever be able to pass. One day she came home crying and her mom looked at her and said, "Alex, you are not stupid. You need to get mad and find a way to learn this stuff. Stay late, ask as many questions as you can. You are smart and you can do this." So that's what she did. She stayed late, asked every question that came to her mind even if it seemed silly. She ignored what everyone else said about her and, when the next report card came, she was the top of her class. Alex was curious and she always knew she was different than everyone else.

As Alex got up to walk towards the house, she noticed her ankle felt completely fine, in fact it felt strong, as if nothing even happened. She tried to keep an eye on Lank but it was too dark and she couldn't spot him any more. She got to the house and hid behind the little shed they had. As she strained to scan the yard to try and see Lank she suddenly got a glimpse of his hair in the bushes. As she crept quietly, keeping a very close eye on the white figure ahead, she began to follow towards the bushes. She even tried to time her steps according to Lank's movement so she couldn't be heard. As she slowly followed, she saw Lank was going up the hill. 'Shoot!' She thought quietly to herself. 'It's a really steep hill made of loose gravel.' Because Lank's feet were so big it was easy for him to climb up, but she was wearing running shoes with slippery soles.

Alex decided to go barefoot up the gravel hill and leave her shoes beside a tree close by. She thought she would have more grip that way to climb the hill. Up, up, up she climbed on all fours, like a mountain lion would. She made sure to go slow and steady while keeping track of where Lank was going. As she got closer to the top, she realized she couldn't see Lank any more — it was too dark and she missed his last few steps while approaching the top dense bush. Suddenly, the excitement turned to fear, when she realized she was potentially making a very foolish decision. She didn't know if Lank was dangerous. He might enjoy eating humans for all she knew.

In contemplation of her safety, she decided to head back down and have a look the following day, when daylight was on her side.

Just as she was about to embark on her journey down the steep hill, she saw Lank again. He was sitting on the top of the hill to the left-hand side beyond the bushes, in what looked to be a narrow grassy path. She remembered going down that path once when she was younger and that there were old cars further down. She thought, 'If I just get a little closer I can see what he's doing.' She crawled up and watched in awe. Luckily the moon was very big and bright, and shining through an opening in the bush so she could faintly see what was happening.

Lank was picking glowing stems, which looked kind of like a mushroom and a flower from the ground. They were glowing bright pastel colors; some were pink, green, blue, and one was white with black spots on it. She had never seen anything like these before and they definitely didn't teach her about them in science class. She thought for sure she would Google them when she got home. In that moment, she saw Lank take a handful of the glowing flowers and shove them all into his mouth at once. Lank took a few steps and reached down to expose an opening which appeared to be some kind of entrance to a tunnel. Lank bent down and jumped down the tunnel, disappearing in front of her very eyes.

She quickly dashed down the hill and ran inside huffing and puffing. Luckily, her mom had fallen asleep on the couch watching TV. She ever so quickly scurried into her room. She grabbed her cell phone and Googled 'pastel mushroom flowers that glow' and 'animals that eat glowing flowers', but she didn't get many hits. She finally found the flower that looked like the ones she had seen, and they were called ghost flowers, otherwise known as *Monotropa uniflora.* They were called 'Indian pipe' and 'corpse plant', which she found fascinating. She read that ghost flowers were rare and not like most plants. They were white and did not contain chlorophyll. Instead of generating energy from sunlight, they relied on trees to grow. They could grow in *very* dark environments, the deep, dark forest being the most ideal place.

As she continued to read more and more about ghost flowers, she learned that, according to a Cherokee legend, Indian pipe plants came into the world as a consequence of human selfishness. The story went that the chiefs of quarreling tribes came together in council to try to settle their fights over hunting and fishing territory. They smoked the peace pipe together for seven days and seven nights. This sacred ritual was supposed to be practiced *only after* harmony was restored, but they chose to not listen. The Great Spirit was angered that the chiefs went to smoke the peace pipe without settling their dispute first. The Indian pipe plant, ghost flowers, were then created, resembling old men with their heads bowed, to remind people to smoke the pipe *only after* they made peace. It was believed that ghost flowers grew only where relatives or friends had quarreled and *still* needed to resolve their differences.

Alex felt intrigued. Curiosity began to drive her crazy as she lay awake in bed, bewildered with enchantment.

CHAPTER 3

It was summer holidays, and Alex was so happy to not have to go to school. She hated getting ready for school in the mornings because her mom would always yell at her. First, she would get yelled at to wake up. Then she would get yelled at to feed her dog, Tobi. *Then* she would get yelled at when the bus arrived. That was three yells before even getting to school. Summer time meant no yelling and just playing.

Alex loved to play with her dog, Tobi, in the summers. Tobi was a ginger cocker spaniel with long floppy ears. They would run around the yard and play on the trampoline. Summer was the best time of the year. Every summer Alex and her mom would go to Mirror Lake to go camping. Alex loved to sneak away when everyone was having fun around the fire, swim to the tall ladder dock in the middle of the lake and lay on the high dock to watch the stars. She felt like she could touch the stars from there. It was the perfect hiding spot. Nothing made her feel more alive, and happy, than that.

Alex's dad was never around to come with them to Mirror Lake, because he worked out of town in Fort McMurray. It made her sad but she was told that if her dad didn't do that, they wouldn't be able to live in

Nelson and she would never want to live anywhere else so she had to accept it. Bev, Alex's mom, stayed at home during the day to take care of her Uncle Willy because he was sick and couldn't be left alone.

Alex's Uncle Willy always thought the radio was saying things directly to him. Her mom would get upset but Alex couldn't help but think it was funny. One time he heard police sirens on the radio and he jumped off the couch and hid under his bed. He locked himself in his room and no one could get in. After hours and hours, Bev managed to break into his window. When she got in, he had pushed his bed against the door and had tin foil over his hat and his glasses. He said it was so the police couldn't track his thoughts. Alex guessed he was stealing all of the tin foil and storing it under his bed. Alex felt mean to be laughing but she thought it was pretty funny when Willy finally came out of his room with a tin foil head.

It was just after lunch and Alex could only think of one thing, and that was finding Lank. She remembered, before she went on her adventure, she would need her shoes that she had left outside. She went to where she last remembered putting her shoes, as she thought she had left them right behind the last tree, before the hill. 'There they are!' Alex ran to her shoes and went to put the first one on. Glancing down, she noticed there was something in her shoe. Looking closer, she realized they were three ghost flowers. One was baby pink, one was baby blue and the other one was white with black spots on it. Did Lank put these in her shoes as an attempt to connect with her?! Alex was bursting with excitement; she could hardly contain herself. Smiling from ear to ear, she rubbed her hands together and laughed out loud. She had seen it on a cartoon once and she always did that when she was excited.

She immediately decided to climb back up the gravel hill to see if Lank was there. Maybe Lank was waiting for her. She started up the hill but wore her shoes this time. She had a feeling this was not going to be a short journey. Higher and higher she climbed in what felt like unbearable heat. She really considered herself quite the athlete, given her less than satisfactory shoes. What other grade five girl would climb a mountain by themselves in this heat? Not many, she thought to herself. Finally, she reached the top and found the same path through the trees she had noticed before, where the old cars were. She couldn't remember exactly where the tunnel entrance was that Lank had jumped through, but she knew it wasn't far from the first car.

"Hmmm, I wonder where Lank would be?" she said aloud to herself. She remembered when she first saw him, he was in the trees. She decided to begin exploring in the trees and thought she should keep a close eye out for ghost flowers because, where there were ghost flowers, likely Lank would be.

As she crept through the trees, she walked straight into a spider web. It actually stuck to her face.

"Ugggghhhh! Sick!" She brushed it off and kept going. With mosquitos buzzing in her ears, out of the corner of her eye she saw a figure move very swiftly to her left. She rapidly looked over to her far left and saw nothing. Then she heard some twigs snap. Someone was definitely there. As she took a few more steps to her left she spotted some ghost flowers—not only a few, but a whole bunch. Straining to see as far as she could, she spotted a figure sitting down. She walked closer and closer, and sure enough, there was Lank. Lank saw her too and didn't move; he just sat there calmly eating the ghost flowers.

She approached Lank slowly and stammered, "It's me... Alex..." in a quiet insecure voice.

Lank looked her in the eye and reached out to offer her a ghost flower. This one was bright fluorescent yellow. She slowly reached her hand out and accepted the ghost flower. As she grabbed hold of it her fingertips glowed yellow too. She felt the sun rays go into her fingertips, just like it had felt when Lank touched her sprained ankle.

As she continued to look into Lank's eyes, she slowly sat down. Lank did not stop her. In fact, he smiled at her with his eyes. As Lank smiled, his cheeks turned pink and the wrinkles by his eyes became very apparent. It was strange because he was smiling, yet his mouth didn't smile; it was just his eyes and the color of his face that changed. In that very moment, Alex knew this was going to be the best summer of her life.

With a closer look at Lank, she noticed his eyes looked like they belonged to a deer, only, around the solid black was a very skinny ring colored fluorescent yellow. His pupils were different from any human or animal she had seen before. They were round in the middle but on the outer edges of the pupils they were pointy. His eye lashes were so long and they grew the longest at the outer edge of his eyes. He had many smile lines on the outside of his eyes, almost like an old Santa Claus. His hair was white blonde and straight, almost as if it was so straight that even in a storm his hair would not frizz or move. It was the thickest hair she had ever seen. His ears were big and floppy; they poked through his white blonde hair. Alex was also struck by how thin his skin was, almost see through, as if it was transparent skin.

Lank did not respond immediately, in fact he looked at her for what felt like an eternity. As Alex waited in anticipation, Lank looked at her with curiosity. Alex painfully endured the silence until she couldn't take it any more.

"My n, n, n, name is Alex, what's your name?" she asked inquisitively.

"We don't have names," he stated in a very deep low rumbling voice.

"What do you mean?" Alex exclaimed.

"Our people don't have names." Alex looked at Lank with a confused demeanor. "We don't understand why you would need a name," Lank slowly stated in his low mesmerizing voice.

"Well… how would you know who each other is?" Alex questioned, as if it was a ridiculous concept.

Lank's face turned pink again. "Why would you need a name for a unique state of existence? Not one single person is the same. No one is like you."

"But how would anyone know you?" Alex asked insightfully.

"How could anyone not know you? You are the only *you* that exists," he stated matter of factly. "You humans forget to use your other senses." Lank paused and sat in silence.

"I don't understand what you mean."

"Energy… humans struggle to acknowledge this entity. Everyone has it and very few use it. It goes hand in hand with intuition."

Alex listened in disbelief, yet she somehow understood what he was saying.

"If you are being your true self and look at someone else with eyes that don't bring judgement, have a heart that doesn't allow blockages, you would be able to use intuition at its greatest."

All of the sudden Alex felt excited. She decided to change the topic. "What are you?" she stated bluntly.

"I come from the Seven Sisters, a star called *Electra*," Lank replied.

"Why are you here?" Alex asked.

"It's a destination, a place I wanted to travel to. A place to exist and learn."

"So how do you speak English?" she asked intently.

"I speak twenty-one languages."

"But why do you want to be here then?" she asked quietly.

"I want to be here because I want to learn about how humans live... and maybe help them see they are destroying themselves and their planet, without even knowing it."

Alex was somewhat puzzled because she thought that the planet was doing fairly well from her perspective.

"Hey, do you want to go on an adventure?" she asked Lank with a twinkle in her eye.

"My existence is an adventure," Lank replied.

"I'll take you to my favorite spot in the whole wide world."

"Sure!" he replied with a pink glow. "Let's take some ghost flowers for the road."

Chapter 4

With all of the excitement, Alex suddenly realized she had to tell her mom what she was doing... well, for the most part. Her mom was a worrywart and always jumped to the worst conclusions. Alex knew she had to get back before the panic really set in.

"Umm, Lank..."

Lank looked down at her with a look that said yes, even though no words exited his mouth.

"I forgot, I have to quickly go do something," Alex stated with an uneasy voice.

Alex quickly ran down the hill, sliding down the gravel parts. She ran as fast as she could to the house and pushed the door open, as she barged in. Her mom looked upset.

"Hey, Mom," Alex stated as she was huffing and puffing.

"Alex, where have you been?" her mom questioned with an annoyed voice.

"I was just exploring, Mom..."

"Well you should have been here to help out. Uncle Willy's not doing well."

"What happened? Is Uncle Willy okay?"

"I have to take him to the hospital. I found out he

hasn't been taking his medications and he is convinced that the government is tracking his thoughts and trying to destroy him. He won't leave his room because he is so scared. This morning I found socks stuffed in the heat register. It could have caused a fire!"

Alex tried not to laugh when her mom said he stuffed socks in the register. But she did know what her Mom meant, this was getting serious.

"Why would he stuff socks in the heat register, Mom?" Alex asked curiously.

"Because he thought the police were spying on him through it," Alex's mom said, rolling her eyes.

Alex tried really hard to hold back a smile and then she felt really worried. She knew it was serious and she really wanted her Uncle Willy to be okay. He was her favorite uncle after all.

"Where's Uncle Willy now? Can I talk to him?" Alex asked quietly.

"Yes, can you get him into the car? I need to take him to the hospital very soon," her mom said, matter of factly.

Alex walked towards his room and her dog, Tobi, followed her. Tobi always followed her wherever she went around the house.

Alex knocked on the door. "Uncle Willy, it's me, Alex." She didn't hear a reply so she opened his door just a crack and peeked in. "Uncle Willy, what's wrong?" she asked in a very concerned voice.

"They're going to get me, Alex," he sobbed. "I'm

so scared."

"Uncle Willy, they won't get you," she replied. "You're strong and it's safe here," she reassured him softly.

"Alex, I don't *feel* safe here though, they are going to get me."

Alex's heart sank when she saw the fear in his eyes.

"Well…Uncle Willy, Mom is going to take you to the hospital so you feel even safer. Come on, hold my hand and I will walk you to the car." Alex put her hand out and looked at Willy with smiley eyes, just like Lank did. Willy looked up at Alex and wiped his eyes. He looked so terrified. Willy slowly reached out his hand and took hold of Alex's as he crawled out from under his bed. Alex pulled him out and walked him to the car.

"Uncle Willy, you're going to be okay. I love you to the universe and back."

"Thanks, Alex, you're my best friend," Willy whispered, as they embraced before walking outside.

"Thanks, sweetie. You better come with us, we will be gone for a few hours," her mom said in her serious mom voice.

"But, Mom, I really want to keep exploring. How about I'll keep in touch and text you. I promise I'll be good."

"Well, I really hate leaving you on your own…"

"But Mom, I'm ten years old, remember. I just Googled it and it says that kids can be left home alone between the ages of ten to twelve…look!"

Bev looked down at Alex's phone with suspicion, "Hmmm... I guess you're right. Well okay, but please promise me you will be careful and responsible. And don't forget to feed Tobi."

"Okay, Mom, I won't." Alex joyfully blurted, trying to sound as much like an adult as she possibly could.

Both Willy and her mom drove away as Alex waved goodbye. Alex ran back into the house, quickly fed Tobi and grabbed her sweater.

"Bye, Tobi. I'm sorry you can't come with me this time," she said as one foot was out of the doorway outside.

Now that Alex had seen her mom and watched them drive away, she flew out the door as she waved goodbye to Tobi. She ran back up the hill as fast as she could without getting hurt. She felt relieved that Uncle Willy was on his way to the hospital and she could not contain her excitement to find Lank. She hoped he was still waiting for her.

Chapter 5

Alex reached the top of the gravel hill, totally out of breath. As she wiped the sweat off her forehead, she called Lank's name loudly.

"Laaaank... where are you?" her voice echoed. "Lank?" There was no reply. "Shoot," she said to herself, "I wonder if he went down that tunnel?" Alex felt really disappointed and actually felt like crying.

"Laaaank." Her voice sounded a bit shaky. She looked as hard as she could, scanning the entire span of the trees.

All of a sudden, Lank came out from behind a tree right beside her. This time he smiled with his eyes and his mouth. His teeth were short and flat. They reminded her of little chicklets cut in half.

"Lank. You startled me." Where were you?" she exclaimed.

"I was here the whole time." Lank snickered a bit.

"Well how come I couldn't see you? I looked with all my might."

"I just changed my composition."

"How did you do that?"

"I concentrate my energy with the tree's energy. I think about being the tree and then I am like the tree."

"So you're like a chameleon?"

Lank's face turned pink.

"Wooooow, I wish I could do that."

"You *can*, you just have to practice."

"Did anyone see you when you didn't want them to before?"

"Not many people pay attention to their surroundings. It's easier here because everyone is lost in their own realities, they barely know who is sitting beside them, let alone someone who walks past them."

"Oh yeah... like my friends don't even listen to me when I talk. They are always texting on their phones," Alex agreed.

Alex suddenly got a burst of energy and she wanted to show off her athletic ability a bit. "Hey, Lank. I'll race ya."

Lank looked at her and took off. Alex had never seen anyone run that fast in all her life. She was running at her top speed and she was still so far behind him she could barely see him in the distance. Alex began to slow down. Before she knew it Lank was sprinting back towards her like a fast sports car.

"Holy. You are soooooo fast," she said with amazement.

Lank wasn't even huffing and puffing. His face just glowed a tinge of blue. She noticed he didn't have any private parts but she was too scared to ask why. He just had a flat area in between his legs and a human-like bottom. She really wanted to know if Lank was male or female but then she realized it didn't really matter, although she had already decided to call Lank a male.

As they continued to walk together through the thick evergreen trees, they approached a divide in the path that went two different ways.

"Which way should we go?" Alex asked playfully.

Lank instantly looked in a direction that didn't line up with either of the paths. Alex decided to just trust and follow to see where it would lead. As they pushed through some thick bushes they came to a cave. A cave she had never seen before.

Chapter 6

As Alex and Lank reached the cave, she could not really contain her excitement.

"Okay, Lank. You go first." Lank slowly proceeded as Alex apprehensively shuffled behind. Stepping into the dark quiet cave, Alex became nervous.

"Lank, what are we doing here?" she questioned.

He looked at her with an air of confidence that made her feel safe. She couldn't see him but she could hear his footsteps. Slowly, she walked forward putting one foot in front of the other, wondering what was ahead, none of which she could predict.

Suddenly, Alex felt static electricity. Like a Bounce sheet being ripped off of a freshly dried towel. "What was that?" she asked with fierce anticipation. Lank did not respond. She began to feel anxious as she tried to reach her hand out to feel something. As she moved her hand, bright colorful sparks appeared before her. "Woaaaa…" Alex was completely bewildered.

"Trust the process, whatever happens, you will be okay," Lank stated calmly. Alex decided in that moment that she could either ruin the experience, or she could stay calm and open. Alex navigated through the dark with her hands and suddenly she felt the static charge getting stronger. She pushed her hand a little bit further and waved her hand back and forth. The air felt very dense and her hand felt as if it had started to move in slow motion. Almost as though she had to force her hand through the air.

"What is that?" she asked with amazement.

"Be still," Lank advised.

Alex stood there in complete darkness, still and quiet like a statue. At once she felt a strong energy, as if someone was standing there right in front of her. A presence of something... or someone... becoming an absolute reality.

Chapter 7

"Lank... who's there?" Alex stammered.

"Alex, who do *you* think is there?"

"Ummmmmmm, well... it feels like a female..." she stated as she moved her hand back and forth through the density.

"What else?" Lank asked in his deep, slow, calm voice.

"I want to call her Loma. She seems really wise and older. Feels very kind and warm, yet strong. *Really* strong. Do you know her?"

"It's someone in my family."

"How come she doesn't talk?"

"She doesn't have to, does she?"

"Oh yeah... I guess you're right."

Alex felt so close to Loma, even after only being in her presence for a short while. She felt so good and comfortable being around her. "I like Loma." Alex exclaimed.

"She likes you too," Lank said with a slight chuckle in his voice.

Alex could hear Lank moving away, heading back out of the cave. "Hey! Wait for me!" Alex yelled.

Alex walked fast so she could grab hold of Lank's

hand. It felt kind of squishy and she looked down and saw both of their hands glowing yellow.

"Wow. Cool." she blurted. "This is the best day of my life." Not only had Alex met Lank, but she also had met Loma which was unforgettable. Alex felt pure joy, until there was a sudden rustle in the bushes that startled them both.

Chapter 8

Alex jumped to her right side, staring at the bushes that were moving around. Lank put his hand out in front of her and signaled for her to be still. Lank slowly crept forward hunched over, looking back at Alex to follow. As they edged towards the bush, a deer poked its head out and stared straight at Lank in the eyes. Lank continued to look at the deer and it seemed like Lank was giving the deer some kind of message. It was hard for Alex to explain but Lank looked like he was focusing on a particular thought or something. The deer put its head down and stopped moving. Suddenly another deer poked its head out. This one was a huge buck with massive antlers. Lank looked at the buck with the same look of intent he had with the other deer. Sure enough, the buck put its head down too.

Lank looked at Alex and said, "Come."

Alex followed Lank and they began walking closer to the deer and the buck. Lank reached out his hand and began to pet the buck. Alex hesitated but she knew that she was allowed to do the same because the deer continued to remain in submission. Alex began to pet the deer. This was such a magical moment for Alex; she had always wished she could pet a deer.

Lank gently put his hand on the buck's antler. Slowly and carefully, Lank got on the buck's back. Alex could not believe what she was seeing.

"Go ahead, Alex," Lank calmly directed. Alex put her leg up but it was a bit too high for her to jump on.

Alex looked at Lank. "I can't get up."

"Ask the deer to kneel so you can get on," Lank suggested.

Alex looked at Lank in disbelief. She had a very hard time believing this would actually work. "Aaaaaahhhh... Mr. Deer, can you kneel down so I can get on?" Alex whispered nervously. Alex couldn't believe her eyes. The deer made direct eye contact with her and then kneeled down. Alex smiled and mouthed 'WOW' to Lank as she got on.

"Hold on tight, Alex. Let's go," Lank stated with a cheeky look on his face.

The deer began to run through the forest at a fast speed and Alex just hung on as tightly as she could, laughing the entire way. Bursts of green and yellow sun flashed, as she looked through the thick, beautiful trees. She had never felt so free. The warm breeze running through her hair felt so comforting and a beautiful sweet smell began to fill her senses.

Chapter 9

The deer began to slow down as the trees became fewer and farther between. Alex sat up, looked into the distance and saw a field that she recognized. "The foxtail field. I *love* foxtails."

As they approached the field slowly, Alex looked down and she could see pink and green surrounding her. The field was so thick she really wanted to roll in it. Alex petted the deer's neck and looked at Lank. "I'm ready to get down."

Lank nodded. "Thank the deer for the ride," he directed.

Alex gave the deer a big hug and said thank you from the bottom of her heart. It was such a special moment for her that she would never forget. Lank did the same and the buck looked like it was hugging Lank back. As they left the deer, Alex was amazed at how many foxtails there were. She had to roll around in them. She felt like she was rolling in a bed of silk, as the tails were long and soft against her skin. Lank copied her and, as they rolled around, they looked at each other and both at the same time burst out in laughter. As soon as Alex heard Lank's laugh, she began to laugh even harder because his laugh was so high pitched and sounded like a bird's cackle. His whole body shook violently, and his entire body turned bright pink. Tears were running down their faces as the contagious laughter trapped them in a state of euphoria. They laughed even harder, until their tummies hurt. Finally, their laughter began to trickle down to a dull giggle until it became quiet again. Alex burst out laughing one last time just thinking about Lank's hilarious laugh. She hadn't laughed that hard in all her life.

Alex grabbed a foxtail. "I love doing this," she said to Lank as she started to brush the silky foxtail against her youthful cheeks. Lank tried to do it too, but his strong, static energy made the foxtail strands separate and hover over his skin like hair on a balloon. The sun's rays felt as though it was a healing power on their faces. As they looked up, they watched and analyzed the clouds in the sky. "Hey, look! That cloud looks like an old man's face." Alex pointed to the left side of the sky.

Lank pointed to the right side of the sky. Alex looked over but she couldn't see anything.

"What is it?" I don't see anything…"

"Look harder," Lank encouraged, "and tell me what you see."

"Ummmmmmm, well… Hmmm," Alex sat in silence for what felt like a lifetime. "Hey. There it is. I see it." Alex exclaimed, "It looks like a bear, a black bear."

Lank looked at her reassuringly as he was proud of her achievement.

"Do you know what that means?" Lank questioned curiously.

"No, tell me what it means."

"It's a message for you. When you cross paths with a black bear it symbolizes a warrior who has strength and confidence. It means you are a leader who will stand against adversity. You will use your healing abilities to help other people."

"Wow. Coooeeeeel. That is my animal. I'm a black bear, GRRRR!" Alex cheered gleefully.

"But there is one other thing you have to remember," Lank warned.

"What's that?"

"It is very important that you have solitude, quiet time and rest, so you can use your strong grounding forces to prepare you for when you are around other people, so that you can help them."

"But that's boring."

"You will need it, Alex, to reach your full healing potential."

"I will try my best. That's the one thing I am not good at, resting."

"You will learn, Alex. I know you will. Did you want to know one more thing that is very special?"

"Yes, of course I do."

"When foxtail fields start on fire, they always grow back because of the special roots they have. Maybe that's why you are so attracted to them, because they are warriors."

"That's so cool. Nothing can keep me down."

"That's right, Alex," Lank chuckled. "Come on, I have something to show you. It reminds me of you…"

Chapter 10

Lank walked a bit in front of Alex to lead the way. His platinum-blonde hair glistened and sparkled. It reminded her of real platinum. She almost had to look away; it was so bright. Alex wished she could trade hair with Lank. Hers was a frizz ball from all of the rolling in the fox tails. She laughed to herself as she watched Lank's ears jiggle as he took each step forward. She had never seen such big ears.

The trees started to get closer together now and suddenly it felt more crowded. There were bushes with yellow honeysuckle and she picked a few flowers off as she walked along, and ate them. Her mom had always told her they were edible. "Lank, where are we going?"

"You will see." The path was getting narrower and hillier. Alex had to duck under some of the branches and climb over fallen trees.

Alex looked down and spotted a really neat surprise, a giant puff ball. "Lank. Look at this!" she yelled at the top of her lungs. Lank slowly looked back. Alex ran up to Lank and as she got really close to him she stated, "Look closer." Lank bent down until his face was almost right up to her hands. Lank had no clue what he was looking at and had a puzzled look on his face.

Alex quickly pushed the giant puff ball together and a huge cloud of puff ball magic dust exploded in both of their faces. Both Alex and Lank coughed a bit and started to laugh. The dark brown puff ball magic dust was all over their faces. Alex noticed the dust was even in Lank's teeth.

"Ha, ha, ha," Alex chuckled. "Sorry." Lank giggled as he wiped his teeth with his long fingers. They continued through the dense forest and it began to feel like a long walk. Alex started to notice her hunger and thirst but she didn't want to be a pain and mention it.

Luckily, right at that moment, Lank announced, "Here we are... Look..." Alex pushed through the last bit of trees and couldn't believe her eyes.

As she peered ahead, she could see a beautiful pond that was so calm, clear and still. It looked like something she imagined in a magazine; a piece of paradise that she would dream of seeing. There were a few giant lily pads in the pond and big rocks that were close to the grass, but sitting in the water. Each rock was placed so perfectly, as stepping stones into the water.

All Alex could see was the brightest, most vibrant color of purple. Mile upon mile of lavender was surrounding her. It was the prettiest view she had ever seen. The fragrance was so strong, every breath filled her with awe. Alex stood there in amazement. She didn't say one word, because she had no words to describe what she saw and felt. Alex began to walk towards the rock path in the water; she couldn't help herself. Lank followed.

Both she and Lank sat on their own rocks. It was so quiet and peaceful. As they sat in silence, admiring the beauty, Alex began to think about her Uncle Willy. She started to worry and wondered how he was doing, if he was okay. Her stomach started to hurt a bit because she was worrying so much. After a few moments, out of the corner of her eye, she got a glimpse of Lank. She noticed his skin had started to change color to a smoky grey color. "What's wrong, Lank?" she asked.

"I feel your worry," he said as his eyes looked into hers with the utmost concern.

"You do?" Alex asked in a quiet voice.

"Yes, Alex, it's very strong."

"Well, I am thinking about my Uncle Willy. He is my favorite uncle and he's not doing so well. Mom had to take him to the hospital. He thinks the government and police are out to get him."

"Worry is black and it causes blockages."

"What do you mean?"

"It stops hope from entering into other people."

"It does?" Alex thought long and hard. "Well… what should you do instead?"

"With love, you encourage and hope."

"Well, what color is that?"

"Light green."

Alex began to smile. "Cooooeeel. Okay, *with love you encourage and hope. With love you encourage and hope. With love you encourage and hope…"* Alex chanted out loud.

As she looked at Lank, sure enough he began to turn a light green color. Suddenly, she understood that her energy could affect other people and she knew she had to remember that in her heart for her Uncle Willy.

Peace and stillness consumed the air. As Alex sat in silence, in the far distance she could hear water trickling. The closer she listened the more she realized it sounded like a large amount of water splashing.

"Lank, do you hear that?" Alex asked Lank quietly.

Lank paused, looking forward towards the sunlight as he thought carefully. "I hear water falling over there," Lank eventually replied.

"Let's go check it out." Alex exclaimed.

Alex and Lank started to walk towards the sound of water, over all of the rocks and eventually along the side on the rocks, following the river. Alex looked into the water and she could see pink salmon, big large groups of them swishing through the river's rapid current but they were swimming upstream. Alex pointed for Lank to see. Lank looked so intrigued. As Alex looked behind her, she could see two black bears feeding on the salmon. Alex knew they were there for her to see in real life, just to confirm what she had already seen that day in the sky. Alex felt like this trip was meant especially for her somehow.

Continuing on, the sound of the water falling was turning into a dull roar. It soon became very apparent they were approaching a waterfall. With much anticipation, Alex and Lank approached a divide in the rocks where they could no longer travel along the moving water without getting sucked in. Gazing ahead as they approached the furthest lookout point they could reach, to the left was the most amazing sight they could have possibly seen. A waterfall, with the sunset in the backdrop. Complete magic unfolding before their eyes.

Lank looked at Alex with appreciation and gratitude before noticing she had goosebumps on her arms and was starting to shiver.

Lank looked at her and said, "I've got to get you home."

"But what about my secret favorite spot I was going to show you?"

"If it's meant to happen, it will, you don't have to worry."

Alex hopped on Lank's back and he ran at lightning speed until they got home.

Before Alex knew it she was staring at the doorstep to her house. She felt her hair and it was so tangled she could hardly put her fingers through it. Out of the corner of her eye she saw Lank slowly walking away towards the steep gravel hill.

"Hey. When will I see you next?" she said as quietly as her voice could go.

"You will know," Lank stated with a glimmer in his eyes, as he slowly turned his head and began walking back up the steep gravel hill.

The look he gave her reminded her not to worry,

almost as if he could already anticipate the future. She felt as though she could completely trust that it would work out. Deep down she knew her mom would be home soon so she quickly ran into the house, ate a granola bar, drank some water and just as she began to brush her teeth, she heard the front door open. Alex stepped out into the hallway to watch her mom walk in, so that she looked super responsible.

Her mom walked in and Alex waved her hand, as she was *really* busy brushing her teeth.

"Alex. Wow, look at you, all ready for bed in your pajamas, brushing your teeth."

Alex shrugged one shoulder, as if it was no big deal, with a half-smile on her face.

Her mom looked really tired. Alex spit out her last bit of toothpaste foam. "Hey, Mom, how's Uncle Willy?"

"Not very good. It will take him a while to get better. He needs to go on new medication," her mom explained. Alex put her head down.

"Get to bed, Alex, we will talk more in the morning."

"Okay, Mom, goodnight."

Chapter 11

Alex woke up to the bright sun shining on her face through the curtains. She could see a robin sitting on the branch, right outside her window. She got up to get a closer look and the robin was staring at her. Its belly was so red and she could see her eggs that were beautiful sky blue, with brown speckles on them. She couldn't believe how a robin with red coloring would plop out blue eggs. She didn't understand why they weren't red.

Alex did a back flop on her bed and then did a backwards somersault. She figured she must have looked like a total champion athlete, as she threw her arms up showing her muscles. She slowly walked up to her mom's door and opened it a crack.

"Mom," Alex whispered.

"Yeaaaaah…" Her mom croaked.

"Is that you, Darth Vader?" Alex asked as she giggled at her mom's morning voice.

Bev laughed as she started to wake up. "What, Alex?" she asked in a humorous voice.

"What are you doing today?"

"I think I want to go camping, to your favorite place. School is going to start soon, so this could be our last camping trip."

Even though it was her favorite place, Alex's heart kind of sank. She knew if they went she couldn't exactly bring Lank with her. How would he know where she was?

"Ohhhh..." Alex stammered.

"You don't sound enthused," her mom stated observingly.

"No... I am..."

Instantly Alex knew she needed to try and leave a note for Lank somehow so he would know where she was. She grabbed her notepad and wrote, *Lank, I am at Mirror Lake, try to find me. From, Alex.*

She ripped off the page and put on her flip flops, "Mom, I'm just letting Tobi out."

Alex quickly ran out the door and sprinted to the same spot where Lank had left the ghost flowers in her shoes. She placed it in the most accurate location she could and grabbed a big rock to put on top of the paper so it wouldn't fly away. She sprinted back to the house so her mom wouldn't suspect anything.

As she got back inside, her mom was already packing. "Get your stuff together, Alex.

Alex packed up her things begrudgingly. "Tobi, we are going to Mirror Lake," Alex yelled. Tobi got excited and started doing laps around the house. It was Tobi's favorite place too because she loved to go swimming in the lake.

They packed up the car and set off for Mirror Lake. Alex was very quiet. She looked wistful as she gazed out the window, keeping an eye out for Lank, in case she could spot him. She couldn't see him anywhere. A tear ran down her cheek at the thought of never seeing Lank again and not showing him her favorite spot.

Alex's mom looked at her through the rear-view mirror.

"You're pretty quiet, Alex. What's the matter?"

"Nothing," she said as she wiped the tear away.

Bev's face appeared concerned and confused as Alex normally would be bouncing off the walls on the way to Mirror Lake. They finally arrived and pulled up to their camp site. They always camped in the same spot every year. They began to unpack and Alex helped her mom set up the tent. She was really good at setting it up because she helped every time they went camping.

Bev knew something was bothering her but she didn't want to push it, so she left Alex alone. Bev had a friend who always camped beside them. Her name was Terry. She would come by their camp site to visit whenever they were both there. Terry and Bev would talk for hours and hours, as they sat around the fire drinking their special drinks. They finally finished putting the tent up and unpacked everything. Sure enough, Terry walked over for a chat.

"And how are we doing today, Alex? " Terry inquired cheerfully.

"Fine," Alex stated abruptly, hoping she wouldn't keep talking to her.

Terry was short and stubby with curly, sandy

blonde hair. She had the loudest laugh ever and she always wore these big black sunglasses that looked like they were designed for professional fishermen.

Alex liked Terry but she just wasn't in the mood for her today.

"Hey, Mom, I'm just gonna go throw rocks in the lake, but I'll be back for dinner."

"Okay, Alex, you have fun."

"Come on Tobi." Alex yelled.

In the distance she could hear a familiar laugh. It sounded just like the kid from school who used to annoy her and tease her. Suddenly she tightened up and felt worried, with the sick feeling in her stomach.

'Oh great,' she thought, 'here we go…'

Alex tried to be invisible. Maybe if Lank could change his color, Alex could turn invisible if she really tried. As she closed her eyes, she concentrated on being invisible. She could hear him laughing and walking closer to her, as she realized it obviously didn't work. Finally she couldn't ignore him any longer so she had to open her eyes. As soon as she opened them, sure enough it was the tall big kid from school, Perry. He had a double chin and a smile that looked like the Cheshire cat from Alice and Wonderland. He had a long dirty rat tail at the bottom of his hair. That especially bugged her. As Perry came closer, holding a football, he took his football and pretended to throw it into her face.

"Ugggghhhh!" Alex muttered in exasperation.

Perry laughed at her as he continued to do fast fake

throws at her face to scare her. He was in her personal space and she hated that.

Quickly Alex called out for Tobi, so she could tell her to go back to the campsite. Perry mocked the way that Alex yelled and repeated it in a baby voice. Alex's face began to burn with anger and her chest got so tight, it felt like she was going to explode. Alex couldn't stand to be around his annoying face any longer.

Tobi quickly followed behind her as Alex made her way back to her campsite while Perry continued to laugh at her. As Alex got closer and closer to her campsite, she could see her mom and Terry talking around the fire. They were being really loud and laughing a lot. Their eyes looked glassy and were half open.

"Alex, dish up. We're having hot dogs tonight!" her mom sang in a loud voice.

Alex grumbled under her breath. This day couldn't get any more annoying for her. She hated hot dogs because they were called wieners and boys had wieners.

Alex quickly ate and decided to have a nap. Hopefully she would dream about adventures with Lank. Camping at Mirror Lake would be made perfect if Lank decided to meet her there.

Chapter 12

A few hours passed and Alex suddenly woke up from a deep sleep to Terry's loud laugh. Alex felt a little bit better and she remembered there was supposed to be a supermoon that night. A surge of excitement sent electrical impulses through her body.

"Hey, Mom, I'm just gonna go watch the stars," Alex informed Bev.

"Alex, be careful and don't be too late, all right?"

"Okay, Mom," she sang as she started running with Tobi not far behind.

"Tobi no. You can't come this time, I'm sorry. Go on." she shouted as she pointed to the tent. Tobi looked a bit sad and walked back to the campsite.

The air smelled clean, crisp and fresh, which gave her the same satisfaction she felt when she hit the bullseye at camp in archery. It was going to be a good night, she just knew it. Alex had read that it was going to be a very long time until another supermoon came. She felt like this year was special for so many reasons.

As she walked past the campsite she finally got a full view of the night's sky. She was amazed at how beautiful Mirror Lake looked. The sky was so clear and bright, she felt as though she could see each and every star and the Milky Way was really easy to see. The moon was so big she could see every grey crater. It seemed like the moon was smiling down at her like an old friend who she hadn't seen in years.

Alex looked around and she couldn't see anyone. It was dark but there was enough light from the supermoon to allow her to see the water and the big evergreen trees surrounding it. Everything was still and the water looked like glass. She just wanted to jump in and mess it all up. Luckily she was wearing her swimsuit. She took off her clothes behind a tree and made triple sure no one could see her. Alex tiptoed into the lake and swam up to the tall ladder dock. It was so high up she felt like she was in outer space. She began to climb up the tall ladder. Up, up, up she climbed until she finally reached the top, out of breath. It was a little cold but she didn't care. Her teeth chitter chattered as she began to lie down and look up into the night's sky. She could hardly believe how stunning the view was and she felt so grateful to be able to be there, alone, soaking it all in.

Alex lay there in silence as she stared at the moon. She started thinking about her Uncle Willy and what Lank had told her to do instead of worry about him. *With love, you encourage and hope.* Alex started saying it over and over as if it was some kind of prayer she was sending out to her uncle. She thought maybe it would help him somehow, some way. She imagined the apple green color as if she was a Care Bear and the color was shooting out from her heart.

At the peak of her concentration, Lank appeared beside her, lying on his back looking at the stars with her.

"Whoa!" Alex exclaimed as she was overwhelmed. "I can't believe you found me. I'm so happy to see you, you have no idea. I had the most annoying day," Alex rambled. Lank just looked at her, smiling while he listened. Alex touched Lank's cheek with her hand. Kind of like a hand hug on his cheek. She couldn't hug him very well while she was lying down. "Thanks for finding me, Lank," she said, with tears in her eyes. Her hand began to glow bright yellow as she touched his face.

"I found you because of the green energy you were putting out. I could see it from far away," Lank said quietly and slowly.

"You could? Amazing." Alex replied proudly. "I was thinking about what you told me to do for Uncle Willy, *with love you encourage and hope*, and that's what I was sending him," she explained.

"Your energy was so powerful, Alex, I know it reached your uncle."

"But how do you know?" she asked inquisitively.

"That's the hope part," Lank stated, matter of factly.

"Hmmmmm," Alex pondered as she considered that possibility.

"Hey, Lank, wanna jump off the dock with me?"

Lank looked at her and gave her the biggest smile as his face lit up bright pink. They both stood up.

"Okay, on the count of three, jump. One... Two... Two and a half... Two and three quarters... Three!"

At once they both jumped off and a big splash erupted as they hit the water. The water felt warm and so refreshing. She loved how her hair felt in the water because it made her feel like a mermaid. As she came up for air she spotted Lank and signaled for him to follow her. Lank swam behind her until they got to the ladder and began climbing up again. When they reached the top they both stood there shivering. Alex could see he had goosebumps on his arms just like she did. Alex put her arm against his to compare goosebumps and they both laughed.

Just as they were looking at their goosebumps, Alex felt something hit her forehead. It hurt.

"Ouch!" she yelled, "What was that?"

Silence pulsated through the air as Alex frantically searched for the culprit. There was no one in sight.

Suddenly, another one hit. This time a rock hit Lank on the arm. Lank didn't flinch but he instantly looked over at the tall cattails in the water where Alex had been sitting earlier. Alex looked over, too. They both noticed the cattails wiggling. It seemed as though someone was hiding in them.

"I bet you I know who it is," Alex said, as her face began to turn red and angry fire began to burn through her chest. "It's that stupid kid, Perry. I just know it,"

Alex fumed. "I am going to give that kid an earful. I can't stand him any more."

From a distance Alex could hear Perry's laugh as it echoed from behind the cattails and Alex's stomach began to churn and her chest got tight. She had the same feeling she got before her dance recitals and she hated that feeling.

Alex turned and looked at Lank. He was watching closely with no facial expression.

"Lank, you should hide. He's going to make fun of us, especially you."

"You should go ask him if he wants to play," Lank replied with kindness.

"What? Why would I do that? He's so mean and he has an annoying laugh. He is always picking on me."

"Well, Alex, you don't know why he is doing that. He is doing that because he feels left out. He hates the fact that everyone enjoys their time around you and not him. He doesn't like that you are having fun and he's not. When you are happy, it makes sad people mad and they want to steal that joy away from you."

Alex thought long and hard. Her heart felt so closed and hurt. After everything she had been through that day and she was finally happy with Lank, Perry had to come along and ruin it. She felt disappointed because she was already having a bad day and this was just another blow. Alex could hardly fight her tears back any more.

"I just can't understand why people want to make me feel bad. I'm doing my own thing and loving other people. Just trying to enjoy myself and I can't. They won't let me."

"*You* are allowing them to stop you enjoying yourself, Alex. It's *your* choice, not theirs. You choose whether or not you let them steal your joy. It's their problem, not yours."

Alex slowly wiped the tears from her face. She knew that it was true, she was giving Perry the power to decide how she was feeling and she realized she didn't want to allow him to make her feel upset. In a flash, Alex jumped off the dock. Alex began swimming towards the shore and Perry walked out from behind the cattails, while he continued to throw rocks at her, laughing the closer she got to him. Alex stood up and looked at Perry in the eyes. She didn't even blink as Perry continued to throw rocks at her. Alex did everything in her power not to cry, but she just stood her ground, looking straight at Perry. Perry started to look nervous, and his laugh began to change to a higher pitched laugh that had no confidence.

"Perry, I recognize you from school," Alex said calmly.

"Yeah, so what, Ginger?" Perry jeered.

Alex ignored his attempt to make her feel self-conscious about her hair. "Perry, you are sad because you aren't having as much fun as us and you are trying to steal my joy and I won't let you," Alex stated in a strong direct voice.

Perry just looked at her, shocked as his face turned

red. He didn't know what to say. Silence filled the air.

"Would you like to play with my friend and I? His name is Lank. He's from another country," Alex asked with the kindest voice she could find without sounding fake.

Perry's facial expression changed. His face went from mean to relieved and it looked like all of his defenses melted away before her eyes. "I would love to play with you guys," Perry replied sheepishly.

"Okay, on one condition," Alex bartered.

"Sure... anything," Perry promised.

"You can't be mean or judge my friend. He's a little bit different but *so* special. You are fortunate to meet him and today is your lucky day."

"Okay, sure, Alex, whatever you say. I won't be mean or judge him. I swear."

"Follow me then," Alex directed.

Alex and Perry began walking towards the water. Perry took his shirt off and jumped into the water after Alex. As they began swimming towards the dock, Alex looked at Perry and smiled. Perry was dumbfounded by Alex's kindness and he hesitated a little bit before he smiled back, almost as if he didn't deserve her kindness.

"Hey, Alex," Perry said as he looked into her eyes. "I'm really sorry for throwing rocks at you," he said remorsefully.

Alex just half smiled at Perry. She still felt hurt in her heart and he had to prove to her he would never do that again to her, but at the same time she forgave him.

They reached the dock and Alex led the way up the tall ladder. As they got to the top Alex told Perry to wait below her so she could ask Lank if it was okay that she introduce Perry to him.

"Hey, Lank," she whispered, "is it okay if I introduce you to Perry?"

"Sure, Alex, if you feel comfortable, then so do I."

"Okay, Perry, you can come up." Alex called out.

Perry slowly climbed his way up to the top, almost completely out of breath as he reached the highest point.

"Perry, this is my friend, Lank… And Lank, this is Perry."

Perry shook Lank's hand as he looked at Lank in utter amazement and slight fear. Alex had never seen Perry's eyes get so big before. As Perry shook Lank's hand it began to glow bright fluorescent yellow.

"Whoaaaaa, trippy!" Perry nervously giggled in disbelief.

Alex had never seen Perry's face light up so much, his smile was from ear to car.

Lank reached out and put his hand on Perry's shoulder and gave him a nod of acknowledgement as he looked into his eyes. Perry felt at ease and completely relaxed.

"I have an idea. Let's all jump off together at the same time, holding hands. I want to show you both something," Lank stated with a mischievous look on his face.

Chapter 13

Alex, Perry and Lank all looked at each other and reached out their hands as they stood side by side.

"On the count of three…" Lank advised.

As they each held hands, all lined up in a row, Alex looked at the supermoon in the background and smiled with gratitude. Alex looked down and she could see that all of their hands were glowing yellow. Although she hoped no one would see them, but somehow she didn't really care.

"Are you ready?" Lank questioned.

Alex and Perry looked at each other and then at Lank as they nodded their heads.

"All right. One… Two… Three."

They all swung their arms to jump. This time the jump felt a little bit different. Alex's feet hit the water and her toes felt really hot. She held on to their hands as tightly as she could. Down, down, down they went until their toes reached the bottom of the lake. Alex's feet got hotter and hotter until suddenly, she felt a pull, as if she was being sucked into a vacuum cleaner. She felt warm sand surround her. It was the best feeling ever, because she felt so safe, like there was absolutely nothing to fear.

She opened her eyes and couldn't believe what she saw.

Chapter 14

Everything was completely still and there was a sense of calm as she slowly looked around. Rays of light entered her visual field as her eyes gradually grew wider.

They were in what seemed to be an underground bubble. Alex looked up and she could see the water above her head, through a circular opening up on the top. Somehow the water wasn't getting inside their bubble.

Alex looked over at Perry and his eyes were so big and blue with his mouth wide open in awe. His smile was literally from ear to ear, as big as the Cheshire cat's grin could get. Surrounding them was every color of ghost flowers imaginable, glowing as if they were glow sticks in the sand.

Alex looked around at the sandy walls. She saw different shaped clear looking rocks embedded in the sand, taking on the colors of the beautiful ghost flowers.

"Oh my gosh," Alex said in utter disbelief.

"Amazing," Perry sputtered, his face appearing as though he was in a state of shock.

Alex looked over at Lank. He sat with his legs crossed and held out his hands to either side with his palms open, facing the ceiling. He looked as though he was radiating rays of sunshine out to everyone. He also took on all of the bright colors that surrounded him and his eyes turned to a white crystal color, similar to the rocks. It was a magnificent sight.

"This is the most beautiful thing I have ever seen in all my life, Lank," Alex gasped as tears began to roll down her face. It was a happy cry. A cry that meant her heart was happy and at peace. She never felt so much love in all her life. It was as if the bubble was filled with such strong love, it was almost difficult to accept.

Perry looked at Alex and began to cry too. He reached out his hands to Alex and put his head down in shame.

"Alex, I am so sorry for all the times I teased you. I didn't know how to be your friend because I have no friends. I was angry that no one liked me and you seemed to get along with everyone," Perry confessed.

Lank reached out his hand and put it on Perry's shoulder. "It's okay, Perry, everyone deserves forgiveness."

Perry put his hands in his face and cried even harder. "I don't deserve that kind of love," he cried.

"Everyone does, Perry. Everyone. Even the meanest, filthiest, cruelest person on the face of this planet does," Lank explained.

Perry slowly wiped his eyes and looked up in disbelief.

"Yeah, Perry, everyone does." Alex smiled and

began to giggle. "Even big fat Ursula off *The Little Mermaid* does." she joked.

Perry couldn't help but give a half smile and let out a little chuckle. "Even the crummy, scummy Cruella Deville?" Perry laughed. "She's the *worst!*"

"Yes, even her!" Alex laughed.

Lank sat quietly and smiled with his eyes full of love and grace towards them both, nodding his head ever so slightly.

"Should we go back up?" Lank asked Alex and Perry.

"Okay," both Alex and Perry chimed.

Lank put both his hands out to hold onto Alex and Perry.

"One... Two... Three."

Instantly they shot up through the water as fast as a bolt of lightning and burst through the top of the water with so much force they sprang out of the water.

"Whoo hoo!" Alex yelled as she did a flip in the air.

"Yewwww!" Perry screamed as he did the biggest can opener into the water.

"Yaaaaahooooo!" Lank hollered as he did a double back flip.

They all laughed with joy as they looked at each other, floating in the water under the beautiful star filled sky.

Chapter 15

Alex, Perry and Lank all lay on their backs in the water, as they looked at the bright stars. They felt so weightless and free floating, without a worry in the world.

Gazing at the stars in a state of contentment, silence surrounded them with peace, like a rainbow after a storm. It was absolutely perfect.

Lank lifted his arm and pointed to the night's sky. Alex and Perry looked to see what he was pointing at. Alex got closer up.

"What is it, Lank?" she whispered as she looked over at him.

"The Seven Sisters," he said slowly with much admiration. Alex was so close to Lank their shoulders were touching. Lank looked at Alex out of the corner of his eye. "That's where I'm from."

Perry floated further away. He was lost in the moment with a big grin on his face in ecstasy as he was staring at the supermoon.

"No way," Alex replied in amazement.

"What's it like?" Alex asked, as she felt so intrigued.

"Come on, I will tell you." Lank began to swim towards the tall ladder dock.

"Come on, Perry," Alex called out.

Perry got up with a sudden look of fear on his face as he realized he was late for his curfew. "I gotta go."

"What? Why so soon?" Alex asked with disappointment.

"My dad is going to kill me, I'm way past my curfew." Perry reasoned with fear in his voice. "I will never forget this. Lank, you have taught me so much, and Alex, you are the best," Perry exclaimed as he quickly swam to shore.

Alex waved goodbye and Lank put his hand out and held it still with a pleased look on his face.

Lank led the way back up the ladder and Alex followed closely behind. Lank and Alex lay on the top of the tall dock, breathless after the climb.

"So what is it like, Lank?" Alex asked intently.

Lank lay there peacefully and looked somewhat baffled as if he didn't know where to start. After a few moments Lank began to speak.

"It's very quiet. We all have an understanding of each other and this life. We are all on the same journey together and that is how we live. Together, as one. Not just one single entity trying to make its way through life like you do here on Earth, against each other, allowing greed and selfishness to control your lives. At the end of your life you all reach the same place, the same consciousness. You will become broken and then you will realize we are all the same and we all need help. In my planet we live with this knowledge and we seem to have understood that sooner than humans. My star is called Electra." Alex felt a little bit puzzled, but she continued to listen. "What's important on Electra is different than what is important on Earth. We have a different understanding of our own existence. We care for our land, and all of its elements."

Hearing Lank say that made Alex remember overhearing her mom talk to Terry about how the world was in a crisis because the ice caps were melting, there had been large forest fires and the animals were dying. She said humans were destroying our planet. Alex wasn't certain exactly why or how, but she knew that her mom thought it was very serious and Terry didn't believe it was real.

"So we aren't taking care of our land?" Alex asked.

Lank looked at her with sadness in his eyes. His eyes turned glassy, almost as if tears were starting to well up. Alex was still as she thought long and hard, trying to understand how we could destroy the Earth and why anyone would allow it to get to this point. It made her sad, and helpless too, as she looked back up to the sky. Alex started to try to imagine what Electra looked like.

"Do you have waterslides there?" Alex randomly inquired.

Lank's face lit up as he looked over at Alex, "If you only knew," Lank retorted.

Lank looked back at the stars as he glowed with appreciation.

"Which star is it?"

Lank pointed to the fourth brightest star at the right bottom of the Seven Sisters constellation. "Right there, Electra," Lank replied with pride.

Without warning, a loud bang went off that sounded like a gun shot. Lank immediately looked at Alex.

"We have to go."

Chapter 16

Alex and Lank quickly climbed down the ladder as fast and quietly as they possibly could.

"Quick, jump on my back," Lank commanded.

Alex grabbed Lank's shoulders and pulled herself onto his back to get a piggy back ride.

"On the count of three I want you to hold your breath," Lank whispered.

Alex nodded fast as she convinced herself she could do whatever it was that Lank challenged her to do next.

Lank counted, "One… Two… Three…"

Alex took a deep breath and they went under the water. Lank swam under the water at an incredible speed to the shore. As they reached the surface Alex took a breath of air. She could have held her breath way longer than that she thought.

Carefully, they came out of the water and Lank put his hands out with his palms facing the sand.

"Stay low," he directed, "do what I do."

Lank began crawling quickly through the sand towards the trees as Alex mimicked him not far behind. Lank's long hair dragged through the sand as he led the way.

As soon as they hit the tree line Lank signaled for Alex to get on his back. Suddenly they could hear sticks snapping and footsteps running closer and closer behind them. Alex jumped on Lank's back and he began to take off. Just as they started running, Alex got a glimpse of a large man running behind them. She couldn't make out what he looked like because it was too dark. Terror gripped the pit of her stomach as she held on to Lank with all her might.

Lank ran as fast as he could through the trees, jumping over obstacles as if they were burning coals. As they raced through the trees the sound of the man began to grow faint. All Alex could hear was Lank's breath.

'Maybe he's gone,' she thought to herself.

Alex closed her eyes tightly as she held on for her safety; she did not want to fall and get hurt or get found by the scary man. The thought of being back at the campsite with her mom wasn't so bad after all. Just then, another gun shot went off. Alex let out a scream, this wasn't fun any more and she began to cry. Lank continued to run through the woods. Alex didn't even know where she was any more. A small twig hit her head as Lank was running and scraped her forehead. She put her head down further into the nape of Lank's neck. Alex had her eyes closed so tightly she felt her head pounding.

Lank began to lose his speed, as he eventually began to tire. At once, a blinding brightness startled them. As Alex looked behind her she saw two headlights and an old Ford truck in the distance.

"Lank, someone is chasing us with a truck," Alex yelled in a state of panic, looking at the bright headlights.

Lank turned around as he continued to run, his eyes widened with fear. As the truck drove closer and closer, Lank spotted a hole in the ground and shouted, "Hang on." Alex held on to Lank so tightly she was sure she was hurting him.

Lank jumped into a tunnel and complete darkness surrounded them as they slid further underground. It felt as though they were on some kind of underground slide. All she could hear was the sound of both of their lungs sucking in and expelling anxious air, as their hearts continue to beat rapidly. "Where are we?" Alex whispered.

"An escape hole," Lank replied with gratitude. "Habasee," Lank cried as he tilted his head up. It was the first time Alex had heard him say something in his language. Alex didn't have to ask what it meant. She knew he was thanking the Creator.

Chapter 17

Silence choked their throats as their hearts continued to pound, uncertain of the unpredictable future. Lank's skin appeared very black. Alex knew what that meant. This time *Lank* was afraid and worried. Alex decided that she needed to lift Lank up somehow, like he did to her that day they were sitting on the rocks in the water beside the lavender fields.

Alex closed her eyes lightly. She took a deep breath in as slow as she could. She exhaled even slower until there was no breath left in her lungs. Inside her head she looked up at her forehead with her eyes closed. She focused right in between her eyes. As she continued to breathe slow and steady, she put some attention on her ears and the sound that was entering them. When she started to think about being freaked out, she just noticed it and then put her attention back to breathing, as she looked through her forehead. She began to visualize light green and the words that Lank told her to repeat, *with love you encourage and hope.* Alex began repeating the phrase in her head while she continued to imagine the color light green. She felt herself floating away, almost as if her spirit was outside of her body, looking down on them in the tunnel. When she looked down, she could see both of their bodies glowing green down below. Alex felt as if she was in that very moment for an eternity. It was so bizarre because it was almost as though she couldn't get back into her body. She wanted to stay there forever and not come back.

Slowly, Alex decided she was ready to come back into her body. She began to feel the sensation of Lank's skin again and felt her ears as she noticed the sound entering them. She wiggled her fingers just a bit to make sure she was still alive. Yes, she was still alive, she reassured herself.

Gradually, she began to open her eyelids. First she could see her eye lashes and then she could see Lank's shining green glowing body in front of her. Alex smiled and felt so proud of her self. She felt strong and brave, like she could do anything she put her mind to. Lank glanced back at her and with smile eyes he whispered, "Thank you, Alex."

Together, they glowed light fluorescent green with absolutely no fear inside of their hearts. Moments passed in this state of bliss as if nothing else mattered in the entire world.

All of a sudden, they heard the deep rumbling sound of a man's voice with an Australian accent. "Where did those buggers go?"

Alex recognized the voice — it was Perry's dad, Gunther. She remembered hearing him shouting when he was picking up Perry from school one day. She could never forget his mean voice and the words he used were always so startling and crass. She knew he was evil the moment she laid eyes on him.

For some reason Alex was still not afraid. She felt so brave, focused and hopeful all at the same time. She knew she was going to get them out of this mess. Somehow, some way. She knew there was *always* a way. As Gunther looked carefully around him he spotted some of Lank's hair poking out of the escape hole. Loud footsteps above the entrance echoed over their heads. Both Lank and Alex closed their eyes.

Chapter 18

"Oohh, what do we got here?" Gunther bellowed as he looked down at the hole, huffing and puffing as if he had just ran a marathon.

Gunther was a rather large, overweight man, who had a double chin and a large belly that hung out of his white tight T-shirt. He wore thick suspenders to hold his pants up and always had a cigarette pack in his shirt pocket. He had a scraggly dark brown beard with dark brown oily hair. His teeth were really crooked and yellow with one gold tooth near the back of his mouth. His nose was always runny, so he was constantly wiping the snot from his nose onto his arm. He was a lumberjack and was known around Nelson for chopping down trees that he wasn't allowed to. Alex thought he was a disgusting man when she first laid eyes on him. She felt sorry for Perry for having such a mean and repulsive dad.

"Ahh, would you look at that," Gunther jeered as he began to laugh. His laugh sounded like a machine gun, fully loaded, as it echoed throughout the forest. "I think I found me a little bunny wabbit," he stated in a sarcastic high pitched voice. Gunther wobbled as he tried to lower down to his knees in an attempt to reach down. His belly was in the way so much he had to fall onto one side. Gunther reached down the hole as far down as his big fat arm could go. Snot was dripping down his nose as he tried to sniff it back up without success. As he reached down he felt Lank's thick hair at his fingertips. "Ah ha." he yelled. Gunther sneered and snickered, as if he had just won the lottery. He grabbed Lank's hair tightly and yanked him up with Alex holding on. Alex held on tightly and tried her best not to cry or scream. She didn't do either and she stayed calm. Lank let out a cry that sounded like a deer when they get shot. "There you are! You thought you could get away from me didn't ya?" Gunther pulled and pulled until both Alex and Lank reached the surface of the ground.

"Don't hurt us, please, don't hurt us," Alex pleaded.

"Naaaawwww, get stuffed."

Gunther pulled Lank up to standing by his hair. Lank grimaced as he endured the excruciating pain. Gunther pushed Lank against a tree and began tying his hands behind the tree. Lank's light green color began to fade, as it started to morph into a smoky grey.

Lank was silent while Gunther pulled the rope so tightly, each pull was like a strong lashing against his back, jolting with each tug. Alex just stood there watching in horror. She couldn't handle seeing Lank be tortured like that. "What are you?" Gunther yelled in Lank's face as he spit while he was talking. Gunther's eyes appeared black with rage. "What are ya, a man or a woman?" Gunther mocked. "Pick a side would ya," he taunted as he cackled in disbelief at what he saw. "What's with the long hair, aye?" he said as he tore a strip out of Lank's head. "Ya dirty mutt."

Lank let out another painful cry as he closed his eyes tight and raised his head to the sky.

Alex couldn't handle watching this any longer. Lank's skin was almost completely black, visibly in despair.

In an instant, Alex had an idea.

"Hey mister, are you Perry's dad?" Alex asked in the sweetest voice she could muster.

Gunther quickly turned his head and set eyes on Alex.

"What was that?"

"Are you Perry's dad?"

"Well, what would make you say that?"

"I saw you picking him up from school one day."

"Well that wasn't me."

Alex thought carefully.

"In school Perry always talks about how awesome his dad is. He said you take him on these amazing hunting and fishing adventures in the Kootenays."

"Ha, ha, ha, well yes, yes I do." Gunther gleamed with pride as he began to smile.

Lank just looked at Alex with hopeful eyes that began to light up.

"I wish I had a dad like you that did fun stuff like

that with me," she stated with a bright and cheerful face with puppy dog eyes.

Without warning, Gunther's entire demeanor changed into a kind, soft-hearted person.

"Oh, sweetheart, where are your parents?" Gunther said with a high pitched caring voice as his eye lashes fluttered.

"Oh... umm... well my mom is just back at the campsite. Dad is at work," she stated slowly as she put her head down, acting as if she was sad and disappointed.

"Well, you run along dear and you go find your mommy."

"Can Lank come too?"

"No." Gunther yelled with rage, as he turned back into the mean evil person he was before.

Alex looked at Lank and Lank looked at her as if to say, '*Go. Run.*'

"Okay, thanks, Mister Perry's Dad!"

Alex quickly ran through the forest as fast as she possibly could. She didn't want to leave Lank but she knew she couldn't help Lank if they were both hurt. Alex ran like she had never run before. '*Please God, keep Lank safe*' she repeated in her head.

Alex finally reached her campsite and as soon as she returned she ran into her mom's arms and cried her eyes out.

Chapter 19

The next day Alex woke up with swollen eyes, she could hardly sleep. She didn't really remember her conversation with her mom because she was so upset. She didn't want to even think about what might be happening to Lank, it was too much for her to bear. As she lay awake in her tent her mom was snoring loudly, she and Terry had a pretty late night. Alex did not know what to do with herself, apart from hang on to hope that Lank would be okay and somehow he would get out of the bad situation he was in. Alex wondered what would happen to Lank if a whole bunch of people saw him. Would everyone start freaking out about aliens or something? This could be so groundbreaking that it could be exposed to the entire world.

All Alex knew was that it was completely out of her control. There was absolutely nothing she could do except to put out the green energy every day as much as she could, instead of the black energy. Trust was a very difficult concept for her because where there was so much uncertainty, how could she trust? But without trust, how could she hope? After going in circles, she decided to make a choice to just hope and trust no matter what. So that's what she did, and she decided to do it with confidence. There are times in life when one has to surrender and see what happens, because control is no longer possible.

Alex grabbed Tobi from the bottom of her sleeping bag and gave her the biggest hug. Tobi was just waking up so she was moaning and groaning, as if she was annoyed at being taken from her beauty sleep. At least she had Tobi with her for comfort.

Alex's mom finally began to wake up as she tossed and turned. The sun began to get hot in the tent, so it wasn't long before they would be forced to leave the tent from sweating so much. Alex's mom slowly opened her eyes.

"Are you okay, Alex? I have never seen you that upset before. You have to tell me what happened, I couldn't make out much of what you were saying last night."

"I was just scared, Mom. I got lost and I got freaked out by this old man who was yelling. That's all. Sorry for scaring you."

"You really worried me, Alex. I don't know if I want you going out at night any more after that. I had no way of finding you either. Why would you go so far? Normally you only go to the dock."

"Well... I don't know... something caught my attention I guess... sorry."

Alex's mom looked disgruntled by the conversation. "Well, let's try to have a good relaxing next part of the trip because you have school coming and I don't want you to be stressed out before you even start."

Alex thought about it a bit. Her mom was right, being at school was stressful enough; being more stressed about Lank, it was not going to help her at all. With that in mind, she decided to take her blow-up dinghy to the lake, and go for a float and lie in the sun. That always made her feel relaxed.

Chapter 20

Lank opened his eyes and looked down at his chest. He could see drops of blood on his chest from his hair being pulled out. As he looked around he wasn't able to see Gunther anywhere. He had no idea where he went or when he left. Lank realized he must have passed out after the trauma of having his hair pulled out. Lank closed his eyes and thought of Alex, hoping she got home safely.

As Lank tried to move his hands, he felt a jolt of pain radiate through his arms. His wrists were cut where the rope was digging into his skin. He didn't even want to see what it looked like. Lank looked all around him and it seemed as though there was not a living creature in sight. Lank could feel hunger and thirst begin to set in. He knew that this was a serious situation and there was not much he could do. Even if he camouflaged into the tree he would still be visible to Gunther because he knew where he had tied him. That would make him even more of a target because it would make him more different than before and he understood that Gunther had a deep hatred for him because he was different.

Lank closed his eyes and tried to begin meditating on the apple green energy. That was the only way he was going to survive this. As he closed his eyes he imagined his home where people understood him. He imagined the happiness he felt when he was with his family and the laughter they shared together. There was no way he wasn't going to see them again, he couldn't allow that to happen. Deep down he knew he had to survive this and he knew that he would have the strength and wisdom to overcome. This situation was not going to defeat him.

As Lank continued to channel his energy, what felt like several hours passed. His stomach was sunken in from not eating and his mouth was so dry he could barely swallow. Lank opened his eyes and the sun was shining bright in his face. He felt so weak that he hardly had the energy to stand.

Just then, Lank heard some rustling in the trees. He looked over and in the near distance he could see a magnificent creature to his right, through the trees. It was very tall, taller than him, and had brown fur that seemed to have almost like a beard at the bottom of its chin. It had the largest body and head Lank had seen on planet Earth. It had very large and pointy things above its head that looked like branches from a tree. Lank wasn't sure what it was but he thought it had such striking features and such a long nose with huge nostrils.

Lank looked at it in wonder and the creature looked back at Lank, right in the eyes. They stared at each other for several minutes. He felt its power and strength just by looking at it. He was amazed at how calm and magnificent the creature was and he had utmost respect for it in that moment.

As Lank peered down in an attempt to *not* challenge it, he felt almost a surrender to the creature as he knew it was much more powerful than he.

Suddenly, a gun shot went off. Lank looked up at the glorious creature. The gun shot went straight into its side, as it fell to its death.

Chapter 21

"Ahh, I see ya didn't get anywhere, did ya?" Gunther hissed with laughter in his voice.

Lank stood silently as he looked up without making any eye contact with Gunther. Lank did not feel safe to talk but he did need to eventually plead for something to eat and drink or he wouldn't survive. "Ya look a little worn out there, freak, don't ya? Your new name is freak, all right? Ya hear me?" Lank looked down at his feet shamefully. "You're gonna tell me where you're from, freak. You ain't getting nothing from me until ya do. Go on, tell me where you're from. I won't tell anybody. What? Ya don't trust me, freak?" Lank continued to stand in silence, frozen with fear and disheartened by Gunther's harsh words. "Listen, freak, do ya want something to eat or what? Tell me where you're from."

Lank did not reply. Gunther got angry and charged up to Lank and kicked him in the legs with such force Lank began to gush pink colored blood out of his right leg. Gunther was wearing steel-toed boots that penetrated straight to his bones, crippling his stance in an instant. "Oh, we're gonna play that game, are we? Okay, well, this'll be fun then, yeah?"

Gunther went to his truck and grabbed his gun and

a large tree stump from the back and placed it right in front of Lank and sat down as he began pointing the gun directly at Lank.

"You're hungry, aren't ya?" Gunther asked with a grin on his face, "You must be thirsty, too, in this blistering hot sun." Gunther got up and walked to his truck to grab a big bottle of water. He walked back and sat down on the stump again. "Mmm, water," Gunther scoffed as he began to pour it over his head. "Oh what, ya want some?"

Lank nodded his head slowly up and down. Gunther stood up and walked towards Lank and poured a few drops on his head.

"Well, you're not getting any until you tell me where you are from, ya feral mongrel."

Lank began to turn almost completely black. He could feel all of his positive energy leaving his body. His eyes began to darken, the yellow was barely even present any more. He was not well and he couldn't hide it any longer. "What are you, you're an ugly thing, aren't ya?" Gunther laughed out loud.

Gunther marched over to the moose and shot it again to make sure it was dead. He grabbed a knife out of his back pocket and stabbed its stomach, as he cut through its thick and bloody flesh.

"Here, ya hungry? Go on, eat it." Gunther taunted as he took a piece of the moose flesh and pushed it into Lank's face.

Lank felt sick to his stomach and vomited whatever

was left in his stomach, which was a few ghost flowers and the remainder of water left in his body. Lank couldn't take the torture any more.

"I will tell you where I am from if you promise me two things," Lank bargained. "Nourishment, and do not tell anyone about me."

"Good mate, I won't tell anyone, I promise. I'll give ya some water and whatever you want to eat, mate, I'll get it for ya. Trust me, mate, trust me."

Lank was silent for a moment as he thought about what he was going to say. He was fearful of the consequence, but at the same time the alternative consequence was death.

"I am from the star Electra, from the star galaxy called the Seven Sisters," Lank replied very quietly.

Gunther did not reply as he made a sarcastic face, somewhat in disbelief. "Good, good on ya, mate. Now, what would ya like for dinner? I'll take you to my place and we will eat. Here, have some water."

Gunther walked over and untied his hands and handed Lank the water.

"Come, follow me," Gunther said in a kind and sarcastic voice. "I'll take care of ya."

Gunther led the way to the truck as he helped Lank in and left the moose in the forest to rot.

Chapter 22

It was time for Alex and her mom to pack up and head back home. Alex's mom was starting to worry about Willy and she needed to make sure things were in place for Alex to start school. Alex helped unpack and take down the tent, while her mom gathered all of the lawn chairs and everything off the picnic table. There was so much garbage to gather around the fire after the party she had had with Terry.

Alex was looking forward to sleeping in her own bed. She really wanted to see her Uncle Willy because he always cheered her up. No matter how sad she felt, he could make her laugh. As Alex began to pack things into the car she noticed a robin again. It felt as though the robin was following her back and forth from the tent to the car. For a second she thought she was going crazy so she stopped after putting a load in the car. Sure enough, the robin flew right onto the car in front of Alex. She was startled at how obvious the robin was making itself to her. Maybe that meant something significant. Maybe it was some kind of sign that Lank was sending her. Alex looked at the robin and it bobbed up and down, almost cheerfully, before flying away. It seemed like either a strange coincidence or a meaningful moment, a message she was supposed to receive. She decided she was going to Google it as soon as she got home.

Soon enough, everything was packed up and they were ready to start their journey home. Alex felt exhausted from all the emotional highs and lows she'd had on the trip. She had never really felt such extreme happiness and extreme sadness all in a short period of time like that. She felt grateful for the experiences that Lank had led her on, and she knew that there was hope for Lank. Something inside of her told her to hang on tightly to that hope and believe that everything was going to work out. She felt a sense of peace take over in her heart. There was no need to worry any more.

Alex slept the entire way home and her mom had a hard time keeping her eyes open during the drive. They were both feeling exhausted. They finally reached the house and by the time they unpacked it was time for an early dinner.

"Alex, I am going to call Uncle Willy if you want to talk to him," Alex's mom informed her.

"Yes, Mom, I would love to talk to him. I miss him so much," Alex stated longingly.

"Hi, Willy, it's Bev here. Yes, we just got home from Mirror Lake. Alex really wants to talk to you… Okay… Yes… Yes… okay, here she is."

"Hi, Uncle Willy!" Alex exclaimed with pep in her voice. "I miss you so much. When are you coming home?"

"Well, they want to discharge me on Tuesday," Willy stated confidently.

"Wow. That's great news. How are you feeling? Tell me everything that happened."

"Well, a lot better actually. I am not so stressed out and I feel safer now. It was really hard at first. There were so many scary people in here and I didn't know who was for me and who was against me. I felt like everyone was watching my every move. I couldn't sleep and I kept accusing people of things they told me that weren't true. I thought I had to protect myself so I was hiding scissors in my room in case anyone tried to kill me. They had to take them away from me and I didn't understand why. I was really sick, Alex. But they put me in a safe area for a while and they changed my medications. My mind feels clearer now and I realize that the nurses are trying to help me. I can come out of my room now and talk to people. I can look them in the eyes now. They taught me how to be confident in myself again. I realized it is not my fault I was that way. It was my illness," Willy explained.

"Whoa, Uncle Willy, that sounds like it was so hard. I am so glad you got through it, I knew you would. Every day I thought about sending you the green energy to help you through it and I kept saying in my head '*with love you encourage and hope*'. It must have worked." Alex exclaimed with excitement.

"Well, I did eat a lot of green apples," Willy stated with laughter.

"Hahahaha. I bet it helped, Uncle."

"Thanks for believing in me, Alex. You will never know how much you have helped me through the toughest times without even knowing it."

"Really?"

"Yes. If it wasn't for you, I don't think I would have even left my bedroom. You were one of the only people I could trust. Thanks for being there for me."

"Anytime, Uncle Willy. You are my favorite uncle in the whole wild world."

"Awe, Alex, I love you."

"I love you too. I'll see you on Tuesday and we can play on the trampoline together."

"Okay, I'll talk to you soon, Alex."

Alex handed the phone back over to her mom and ran into her room so she could grab her phone to look up what it meant to see a robin. Alex was excited again and felt a jolt of joy spring through her body. She felt happy again and her heart was full, just like it was when she was with Lank. She felt like crying because she was so overwhelmed with gratitude that her Uncle Willy was better. She had never heard him sound so good in years. Her hope really had worked.

As she jumped on her bed, Tobi wasn't far behind as she curled up right beside her in the nook of her legs as she lay on her side.

She grabbed her phone and Googled 'what does it mean to see a robin' and this is what she found:

A robin signifies stimulation of new growth and

renewal. The robin teaches that any changes can be made with joy, laughter and a song in your heart. They show you how to ride the winds of passion within your heart and become independent and self-reliant through this change. The robin will teach you how to move forward.

As Alex read the meaning, she instantly thought about going back to school. She felt like this year there was going to be a change for her in her heart. She felt like she was going through new personal growth and renewal. She already sensed this since she met Lank. She had more joy, laughter and song in her heart and she could take that with her when she went back to school. It was so perfect to her that it was as though the message was given specially to her from the universe. She couldn't be happier in that moment and felt excited about the school year, instead of the fear and worry she felt before. She couldn't wait to see what else this year was going to teach her. Now all that needed to happen was for Lank to be free and safe from Gunther's hands. And if her green apple energy had helped her uncle, she knew it could help Lank too.

Chapter 23

Lank found himself in the cellar at Gunther's farm, alone and cold. He drank lots of water and ate some kale, spinach and brussel sprouts that Gunther gave him from the garden. Even though he was fed and not thirsty any more he didn't trust Gunther's word. He felt like he was not quite safe but all he could do was wait and see what would come his way next.

Lank's body was still very black and the yellow color was no longer shining in his eyes. He was in complete darkness and it was cold and lonely in the cellar. Lank tried to meditate until morning, but he didn't have the strength to. He felt as though he had nothing left in him, no energy, no hope, just emptiness. He knew the Creator was still there but he just felt so alone. He had never been treated so badly and it really beat his spirit down.

Lank was used to having only supports around him, people who encouraged him and brought him up. He was used to only being around other people with green energy and he had never been around the black energy for very long. He was always able to turn it around for other people, but Gunther's energy was so dark. He had never witnessed black energy so strong. All of the negativity and abuse made him second guess himself.

'Maybe I'm not special. Maybe I'm not on planet Earth for a good reason. I haven't done much so far to help the human race. All I did was play in the forest with Alex, which only served myself. Maybe I was selfish for doing that when I could have been helping people who were really in need. Alex wasn't in need at that time. She was doing well. I should have paid more attention to what I should have been doing. I am so terrible and useless. And now I have ended up here, in this situation. I deserve to be here and to not get out. I deserve to die.' Lank conversed in his head to himself.

Lank began to cry. His tears were a very deep dark black. He had never seen his tears black before. He knew he was not in a good place and he needed help to survive. He couldn't do this alone.

***

The next day arrived and Lank had gotten very little sleep. He woke up to a loud bang where the opening to the cellar was. The door opened and the light that entered was blinding; Lank could hardly see. All he could hear was loud laughing and a group of men talking to each other as they made their way down the stairs.

In entered five older men, all staring at Lank with amazement.

"What in god's name is it?" Gunther's friend asked

in a bewildered voice.

"He must be some kind of alien."

"Well, he is from the stars apparently," Gunther laughed, as he informed his friends.

"What a crock!"

"You must be kidding me."

They all circled around Lank and poked and prodded at him without respecting his personal space. Lank felt like an animal in the zoo. He was right, he couldn't trust Gunther one tiny bit.

Lank just sat there with his head down and didn't fight back. All he could do was ask the Creator to give him love for them. It was the only thing he could do in that moment of absolute weakness and surrender.

"We should show him to the news reporters and get a bunch of money for exposing the first real live alien."

"Yeah! We could make millions."

"I am already planning on doing that, ya bunch of dimwits, don't even think about stealing my fortune. I'm the one that caught the dingo," Gunther stated with a sense of entitlement. "I earned this and deserve every penny. Now get out of here guys. And if I find out any one of you have let the secret out, I'll kill ya. Every one of yas!"

Gunther's friends became somewhat threatened, as they all became quiet and nodded their heads in obedience.

"If you keep your mouths shut I'll pay you each a little something, I promise," Gunther ensured.

Lank had an awful feeling in the pit of his stomach. He felt as though something terrible was going to happen. He wasn't sure what, but he knew it wasn't good.

Chapter 24

Darkness filled Lank's existence once again. There was nowhere to go, nothing to eat, no drink, and no opportunities to get out. All he could do was close his eyes and keep himself in a calm state. He felt as though there was some sense of peace because he realized he was not going to allow himself to be there forever and the worst thing that could happen was that he would die, and Lank did not fear death. In fact, in Lank's culture when they passed on, they stayed the same but just turned into Loma's form. Even if they tortured him more, it was only going to be temporary pain. This was the only thing that Lank could truly hang on to.

Days passed and Lank remained in the same place in the deep dark cellar. There was no one to rescue him. No one to make him laugh. Just silence and time. Lank knew it wouldn't be long before the door opened again because he knew they wouldn't be able to contain their curiosity and it would be difficult for them not to tell anyone. They wouldn't want him to die yet, without any reward.

Sure enough, the door opened and blinding brightness penetrated his soul in a startling fashion. He heard a loud thud and down came Gunther, who was thrown into the cellar. But this time was different. None of his friends followed.

"Let me outta here, ya bunch of traitors!" Gunther shrieked aggressively. "I can't believe they've done this. These are supposed to be my friends."

Gunther began pounding on the cellar door with such force Lank thought the door was going to smash open. Lank didn't know why Gunther was down there with him and how things were going to play out. Gunther was upset and fuming; he didn't have anywhere to go, nowhere to escape to. Absolutely powerless, at Lank's mercy. There was nothing he could do as he sputtered in anger and paced around the cellar in the unescapable darkness. Gunther began to cry as he gave up and fell to the ground. Gunther was sobbing and his rage seemed to dissipate into sorrow. Lank could not help but begin to feel some compassion for Gunther. He knew the cry of desperation and that was exactly what he was hearing. Lank understood that every living creature is brought to that place where they cry out and need help of some kind. Anything in that moment to relieve them even a little bit from the desperation would help.

As Gunther began to cry, Lank reached out his hand and placed it on Gunther's shoulder without saying a word. Gunther just wailed and wailed as he felt entirely hopeless and helpless.

"Why would they do this to me? I thought they were my friends and they took advantage of my kindness. How could I be so stupid?"

Lank remained quiet and focused on compassion and empathy for Gunther.

"I'm gonna be left to die in here, aren't I?" Gunther stated with no sign that his tears were going to stop running down his face.

Gunther was absolutely terrified of death. He didn't know what was going to happen after he died and ever since he was a little boy, he had feared how painful he imagined death to be. He'd always feared dying in a car accident and he'd had nightmares nearly every night when he was a young kid. When he would get upset, his parents would not console him and would not come to protect him or talk to him. Instead, he was always left alone to cry and ever since he was paralyzed with fear about death and dying. Gunther had a strong staunch exterior, but deep down inside he was a frightened little boy who had nowhere to run to. That's why he was always a big bully to others, because he wanted to scare other people away so that they wouldn't challenge him. If he was challenged then he wouldn't know what to do with that. So instead, he scared other people first. For the most part it worked. Most people avoided him and laughed nervously around him. They weren't sure what he would do next or when he would snap. He was very unpredictable and unpleasant. His most famous move was the 'making people feel stupid' tactic. He would laugh at people if they asked a question. Even if it was a good question, he would laugh at them to make them second guess themselves. He especially loved to belittle people. He was very good at that. All it took was a squinted look of the eyes or a scoff in his voice that would instantly dismiss what someone was saying. If the person would stand their ground then he would up his game by starting to call them names and make fun of how stupid a question it was. They would almost always go away after that.

Gunther felt good about himself when he made people feel stupid and sheepish. That was what he lived for. He even did it to his own son, day after day. He was very drawn to weaklings, in particular really nice people, because they were the easiest target to fuel his low self-esteem with such satisfying doses of misinterpreted self-confidence. He didn't care if he got the upper hand when he shouldn't have. He always said to himself that if the other person didn't beat him to it, they didn't deserve to win the conversation because of how weak they were. He didn't care about what was right or wrong, true or not true; as long as he was made to feel better at another man's expense, he was all over it.

This actually worked well for Gunther most of his life. He was always on top. And even if someone second guessed him, they would always end up second guessing themselves instead. Another act that Gunther loved was bulldozing. He was very talented at that. He would talk louder than everyone else, interrupt people's conversations and blurt out answers before anyone else could so that he could be noticed first. He had to have the answers first. This was a great skill of his as it took a very long time to perfect. Over time though, he found that most people wouldn't challenge him or redirect him by informing him he rudely interrupted. He found that most people would slump over in their chair or withdraw from the conversation, which was great, more time for him to take over. People actually would go to him for the answers because he always had the answers. Even if he was making the answers up, he had the answer, and he didn't care. He was an expert on everything. A 'genius' some might say. He was a jack of all trades and could converse from topics such as politics, to topics about how to become a millionaire, how to fix trucks and sports cars, all things he knew *nothing* about. He loved to outsmart his friends who actually knew about these topics. His trick was to actually learn from them first and then use their information to make him sound like he knew what he was talking about. Even though they were the ones who knew about the topic, given it was their career and all, he would answer questions for them when other people would ask. And not only that, he would actually educate the person who was actually the expert about the topic they know everything about. It was great.

Gunther was also an artist when it came to making people feel bad about themselves. He loved to evoke in people feelings of guilt, shame, insecurity, failure, fear, and best of all, self-doubt. He was very crafty and paid attention to any sign that someone had a particular weakness or insecurity and he would play on that to the largest extent. If someone mentioned they had a zit on their face, he would really look at it and then begin recommending different types of solutions to treat severe acne. Or he would notice that someone wasn't sure about the new shirt they bought and he would comment to them about how it didn't go with what they were wearing. When he got really good at it, he would disguise playing on the insecurity by telling them in a very nice and concerned voice. He would try to artificially instill trust in these people, telling them they could tell him anything, and then use that to his advantage. He was no fool. He was so intelligent and talented at this act that he fooled several people. And the ones he couldn't fool, well he stayed far, far away from those ones. He could not chance getting hit up about his behavior or put in his place. No, he wouldn't be able to manage that.

It took a lifetime for Gunther to fully develop these tactics; in fact, he didn't become professional at this overnight. It took many many years of practice and many burnt relationships before he could truly get people under his control. But he found a way.

Gunther did not like when other people would succeed. At all costs he would put down others' successes, drown them out or discount the value in them. After all, their successes weren't important to him. Their failures were and that was much more worthwhile to spend time on. He hated talking about himself, because that would take time away from focusing on what was wrong with the other person. Gunther didn't show vulnerabilities. He didn't trust anyone. He thought if he showed vulnerabilities that other people would be smart like him and use them against him. Only a weakling would talk about their struggles. But not Gunther. Gunther was very 'wise'.

Gunther took pride in being selfish. This was what fueled his core and influenced most of his other acts. Without selfishness, he would have to be self-less, which was completely not an option in his mind. Put himself first *always* was his mantra. Because if he didn't, well who would, right? This world was about him and he needed it to be that way because if it wasn't there was a very high risk he could lose it all and people would find out he was a phony.

As Gunther sat there and cried it was the first time he cried from powerlessness since he was a young child. He did not know how to sit with that kind of pain.

Chapter 25

Lank knew how terrible Gunther was but he also could
see straight through it and figured it was a sad way to
live. It seemed so exhausting, behaving the way Gunther
did. No relaxing or letting go. No trusting or
surrendering control over to the Creator. Trying to
always be in control was a very difficult feat in Lank's
eyes. Lank didn't see it as even possible to try taking
that into one's own hands and, if tried, it would be a life
of persistent stress and agony. Lank felt sorry for
Gunther because Gunther could not be alone with
himself. Gunther needed to run from everything to
avoid being still within himself. Lank knew how
horrible that must be, not being able to face yourself and
be honest or look at the pain. The more Gunther
avoided, the more unhappy he became until he broke
down that day in the cellar.

"Some food or drink, Gunther?" Lank asked softly.

"I'm extremely hungry and thirsty too," Gunther
replied as he wiped the remainder of tears off his face.

Suddenly, Gunther remembered there were
potatoes in the cellar that he left to keep fresh and a jug
of water close to the old spring mattress too. He got on
his hands and knees and began to feel around on the

floor to find the latch to the potato storage room. As he reached and felt around he finally felt the latch and reached down, through spider webs to grab a hold of some potatoes.

"Here, mate, here ya go. Have a potato. It's not much but it'll tide you over," Gunther advised.

Lank, without hesitation, accepted the potato and took a big bite. It sure didn't taste very good but something was better than starvation. Gunther reached around the mattress to try and find the jug of water he thought he left there. He moved his hands in all directions but could not for the life of him find the jug.

"I can't find the blimming jug anywhere. I know I left it here somewhere. Hey, can you help me or what? Don't just sit there and stare. Get off your backside, and look."

Lank had an idea. "Gunther, if you touch my hand it will create light so we can see the jug."

"You gotta be kidding me."

Lank reached out his hand and slowly, Gunther put out his hand. At this point, he had nothing to lose.

As they reached out for each other's hands, finally they touched and a bright fluorescent glow appeared before their eyes.

"Well isn't that amazing," Gunther blurted out without thinking.

As they looked around the room, they spotted the water jug.

"There it is." Gunther exclaimed, "Come on, move

slowly beside me, would ya?"

Carefully they both crawled to the water jug while continuing to touch hands. Gunther grabbed the jug and skulled almost all of the water but kindly saved Lank less than a quarter of the jug; he was feeling awfully generous in that particular moment. Lank was grateful for even one sip, so he thanked Gunther sincerely for his generosity. Together they sat, hand in hand eating potatoes in the cellar. This was the best moment they had ever shared and Gunther appeared awfully happy and content.

Chapter 26

It was time to get ready for the school year. Bev, Willy and Alex decided it was time for a clean-a-thon. Every season they would have one and it was always so much fun. They would blast their favorite music and clean the house top to bottom while they ate their favorite snacks and drinks. Alex thought it was the best way to clean because they had to do it together and they always had lots of laughs while they did it. Alex got to pick the first song and she decided to pick the song *September* by Earth Wind and Fire. Her Uncle Willy introduced that song to her and it always made her happy and energetic. Alex cranked the volume and grabbed the vacuum cleaner. She liked to vacuum because she felt strong and grown up when she did that chore. She loved to sweat and feel like she was doing a really hard job.

Willy's favorite chore was collecting the cups. Alex always thought it was the funniest job because it was barely a chore. But it did need to get done because there were always empty mugs in her room and in Willy's room, not to mention behind the couch and on the coffee table.

Bev always chose dusting because she didn't think Alex or Willy could do it right. Alex didn't understand why you couldn't just go around objects and why you had to remove them? Her mom made it way harder than it had to be.

Alex started doing her wiggle dance where she would wiggle each leg that stepped forward to push the vacuum while she shook her head. It must have looked funny because her Uncle Willy would always laugh out loud hysterically while she did it, which always made her happy.

Willy's dance made Alex laugh because he only used his arms, going straight out and in as he held mugs in his hands. It wasn't really a dance but she knew Willy was trying.

And Alex's mom's signature dance was where she would push her butt out and bend her knees to the beat of the song. When she got really into it she bent her elbows in a funny fashion to make Alex laugh even more. Those were her most favorite times with her family, even though they were just cleaning. Her mom knew how to make everything fun and funny.

It didn't take long for the place to look spick and span and they all felt like they got a good workout from all the moving and laughing. Alex was pouring sweat by the time she was done.

"Alex, do you want to go shopping for some back to school clothes?" Alex's mom inquired.

"Well, I guess I should..." Alex said with some dread in her voice. Alex hated shopping. It took so long and her feet always hurt. It made her feel trapped and

Alex hated feeling trapped. She only liked feeling free. But she did know, deep down, that she only had one pair of pants and two shirts she actually liked, and wore every single day.

Alex, her mom and Willy hopped in the car and drove off to her favorite store in Nelson. It had all kinds of hippy clothes in it, which was exactly what she liked. She hated wearing what other kids were wearing. Alex tried on several items and her Uncle Willy and Mom got to play judge. She tried on all sorts of colors and crazy patterns. None of them seemed to really suit her until she found this awesome jumpsuit. It was perfect because she only had to put one thing on and it looked like it was from the seventies. It was maroon velvet with a hood and flare bell bottoms with a long zipper in the front. No one would have that, she was pretty sure. As soon as she got out of the dressing room she did a dance like an Irish leprechaun's jig. Everyone laughed and clapped, telling her it looked awesome.

Alex was more ready than ever for school and what the year was going to bring. The only thing left was finding Lank. Her heart told her that she was going to see him soon and she didn't doubt that for one second.

Chapter 27

Blinded by light, both Alex and Gunther were rudely awakened by people barging into the cellar. This time it was only one of Gunther's friends, Jimmy.

"I think we got a reporter who wants this story. I came to warn you that the other guys are plotting against you and want you dead, Gunther. They don't want you to get the money and fame from this," Jimmy warned in a panic.

"I don't believe you, Jimmy. They wouldn't dare do something like that to me. You're full of crap, aren't ya?" I am going to release the story and I don't care if Lank is dead by the time I bring him to the public eye," Gunther stated defensively, with no consideration at all for Lank, "This dirty little waste of space is going to make me my millions, I assure you that."

Lank's heart sank. He had thought there was a chance Gunther had warmed up to him but it didn't appear to be that way.

Jimmy got angry and stormed out. Before he left the cellar he yelled, "Then go ahead, and go stuff yourself, Gunther," and he left without turning back.

Chapter 28

Gunther held his stomach in pain from all the potatoes, as he drifted into a deep sleep. His snoring sounded like the trembling of an earthquake. Lank looked around him, pondering how he would ever escape the nightmare he had entered. Lonely and desperate, Lank scanned every corner of the cellar. He looked closely at the entrance to see if there was any weak spot he could bust open. There were dead bolts on the outside and he couldn't bang too hard or else Gunther would wake up.

As Lank gave up on that option, he peered into the deep dark corner that he had not paid much attention to. As he crept slowly and quietly he saw some old potato bags against the cellar wall. Lank pushed them away and as he did, his hand knocked on what felt like a door knob. Lank quickly tossed the bags and tried to feel his way around the darkness for the door handle. Sure enough, he grabbed a hold of it and slowly turned the door knob. As he quietly opened it, he realized it was a mini door that barely grazed the height of his knees. Lank crouched down and peered through but all he could see was complete darkness. Lank looked back to see if Gunther was watching him but luckily he was still sound asleep. Lank thought carefully of his next move.

Should he push his head through the dark doorway to see where it led? Or should he wait for an opportunity to escape some other way? In contemplation, Lank felt there was nothing to lose. With that he began to poke his head through on his hands and knees as he began to crawl forward. Spider webs plastered his face, as he crept further into the black abyss. Lank squeezed his shoulders through the doorway and then his torso and legs, as he got into the tiniest, most awkward position possible, scraping his back as he pushed through on his hands and feet. He crawled until he had completely entered. Nervously, he turned around, reaching to close the door behind him so Gunther wouldn't notice when he woke up. Lank shut the door, hands trembling, throat dry. Fear and relief encompassed him at once, when suddenly a brief flash of bright light blinded him, so fierce he could not see anything. The only thing Lank could feel was a strong pull of gravity dragging him down with such force no amount of strength in the world could stop him from accelerating down.

Chapter 29

Alex's first day back to school was not as amazing as she had envisioned. She had to sit by a girl named Kristen. Kristen had always annoyed Alex last year and today was the absolute worst. At recess she was bragging about how she got her period over the summer and would not stop talking about it. Alex thought you should be embarrassed about it or at least keep it to yourself. Kristen thought she was so smart. She was constantly correcting Alex in class every time she tried to talk and then made jokes to the other girls about Alex not 'getting it' in a pretentious, scoffing manner. Alex felt left out and alone the entire day, like she didn't belong anywhere, including sitting alone by herself. She felt so exposed, like she just wanted to go into the bathroom to hide.

After school, Alex was on the bus home, leaning against the window watching the grassy ditch pass by as she began dreaming about Lank. She started to wonder if Lank's sister, Loma, was still in the cave up the hill from her house. Maybe she would have some answers or guidance for her, maybe a sense of comfort after such a bad day. Instantly, Alex became happy and excited at the thought of finding Loma. Alex moved to the front seat of the bus so she could run out and get to the cave as fast as she possibly could.

Chapter 30

Gunther woke up from his deep slumber, wiping his eyes and yawning. He had slept for so long he forgot where he was, only to soon realize he was still trapped in the cellar and his sore stomach had not gone away. Gunther looked around and noticed Lank was no longer there with him. Frantically Gunther yelled, "Where did that greasy little maggot go?"

As Gunther scanned the room, he saw that the potato bags were moved and he noticed a little door. Gunther laughed in anger, as he neared the door. "What a piece of work." Gunther sneered with gritted teeth as he turned the door knob quickly, opening it with force. To Gunther's dismay, all he could feel was an empty small space that looked like it was meant for potato storage. Gunther was confused and filled with rage. He felt like he was going crazy and began yelling and banging his head against the wall. Gunther started to fear he would die alone in that cellar, with no one to hear his cries, which was one of his absolute worst nightmares.

Chapter 31

As Lank opened his eyes, all that surrounded him was complete and total darkness. He felt sick to his stomach as if he had fallen thousands of feet in an instant. Completely weightless, Lank had no idea where he was. As he opened his eyes, flickers of light began to appear, almost as if he was trapped in a tunnel with thousands of stars passing him at an insanely fast pace. When he finally realized he could not fight this experience, he let go to see what was potentially being revealed to him.

Lank realized he had no control over what was happening. As soon as he surrendered, he saw an image of a Cherokee man, wearing a head dress. He didn't know what it was but he began to cry at its beauty and strength; he couldn't speak. As Lank looked closer, the man appeared to have bright blue eyes. As he looked even closer, he could see planet Earth in each of his eyes, as if someone had taken a photo from outer space and placed that photo in his eyes.

"My people and my land have been forgotten. Destruction of Mother Earth is near." His voice made Lank vibrate all over. Lank began to see beasts appear — a moose like the animal he saw Gunther shoot. A black bear, like the one Alex saw. Deer, cougars and mountain goats all began running at high speed towards him. Every animal he saw in the forest began running rapidly towards him. Startled and afraid, Lank began to scream in fear of them trampling over him. As they drew closer and closer they suddenly began to lose their strength and their feet began to shatter and dissipate. The closer they got to him the faster they disintegrated before his eyes into a gold dust that surrounded him. Lank could hear the cries of each beast as it crawled towards death.

Then, as he looked beyond the gold dust from the beasts, he saw a massive tidal wave coming towards him. Panicked, Lank attempted to escape but there was absolutely nowhere for him to go or to hide. Faced with the tidal wave, Lank accepted defeat and it swallowed him whole. Desperately struggling under water, Lank was losing his breath. As he looked up towards the break, kicking with all of his might, he began to feel faint. Finally he caught some air as he gasped above the water's surface. Lank caught his breath and coughed for survival as he looked around him. All Lank could see for miles was floating fish. The stench was unbearable. The water was so hot, he could hardly handle it; he felt as though he was in a pot of boiling water. In sheer desperation Lank began to yell at the top of his lungs for help. There was no one in sight to save him. As he pushed through the thick piles of fish, his body was covered in fish guts and slime. At that moment Lank looked up and spotted a small rock poking out of the water in the distance. Frantically he swam for safety towards the rock. As he reached the rock he realized this was the only thing in sight that could temporarily save his life. Lank grasped the rock as tightly as he could, as he slowly pulled himself up.

Lank sat on the rock and looked towards the distance. All he could see was the sun, which was extremely dim. He could barely see the shape of the sun. Finding his stability, all he could hear in the distance were cries; this time human cries that were unbearable to hear. Desperation was heard in the distance and all Lank could do was close his eyes and pray for some kind of escape from this abhorrent, loathsome, nauseating experience.

Chapter 32

Alex finally reached the familiar cave where Loma lived. As she entered the cave, she began to feel the same static she had felt before, so she knew Loma was there. As she got further and further into the cave she waved her arm to see what she could feel. Her hand moved slowly, even though she was moving it as fast as she could.

"Loma, are you here?" Warmth and peace began to surround her. "Loma, I have lost Lank and desperately need to find him." Loma did not mutter a word but as Alex waited in silence, she began to see a pink glowing light beam in a line towards her heart. Alex began to feel flushed and slightly dizzy until the beam disappeared and she felt calm, strong and confident, almost as if she knew exactly what to do, even though she really didn't.

"Thank you, Loma. I can't explain how you've helped me." Alex knew exactly in that moment where she had to be.

Chapter 33

Lank held his ears and began to cry. As he closed his eyes he remembered that he had to channel his green energy to help him through this. As he began to visualize it, he started to repeat the verse he held close to his heart that he shared with Alex, *with love, you encourage and hope*. As he repeated this, suddenly he began to feel hot and a strong pressure. He was pulled again into a starry dark tunnel that pulled him with the strength of super charged gravity. As he opened his eyes and looked up he could see the opening of the well which looked strangely familiar. As he began to try to climb up the well, he saw a shadow above him. With anticipation, Lank called out, "Can anybody help me?"

The shadow got larger and lo and behold Alex's face appeared looking down upon him. With sheer disbelief they both began to laugh and cry.

"I can't believe you are here. You saved my life. How did you find me?" Lank exclaimed as he was overwhelmed with relief.

"Loma, somehow showed me. And I used my intuition," Alex replied, with such joy and pride that visiting Loma had been the answer.

As Alex began to look down beside the well, she

saw a rope. How the rope got there she had no idea but she knew exactly what to do. She figured it must have been Loma's doing. Alex began to let down the rope and Lank was glowing the brightest fluorescent green she had ever seen. His face was pink as he was so relieved and happy to see Alex.

As Lank gradually climbed up and reached the opening, he finally was able to place his feet on solid ground. Just as he reached out to give Alex a hug, the ground began to shake with such power and vengeance, they both fell to the ground as a loud crack and rumble filled the air.

Chapter 34

The earth was shaking violently, as Alex and Lank held on to each other. All Alex could think of was her mom, Tobi and Uncle Willy. The earth began to split in front of their very eyes but luckily they were standing in the right spot where the earth didn't divide. Terrified, in a state of shock, Alex and Lank held on to each other tightly as trees began to crash around them. Miraculously, no trees landed on them. The ground continued to shake for what seemed like an eternity, until finally the earth came to a rest.

Lank looked at Alex and turned his back, which Alex knew was an indication for her jump to on. Alex jumped on Lank's back and he began to run. He ran through what felt like a war zone. As they drew closer towards Alex's house, suddenly they came into contact with someone they both knew.

Chapter 35

Bev couldn't believe she was still alive as she pushed aside the rubble left over from what used to be her house. Willy was shaking behind a fallen tree, speechless and terrified. Tobi was not far behind, shivering. As Bev walked towards Willy, they both started to cry as they held each other tight with disbelief that they were both still alive.

"It's going to be okay," she reassured Willy.

"But what about Alex? She could be dead out there," Willy said through his overflowing tears.

Chapter 36

"Help. Help. Please someone, anyone."

In front of their very eyes, Gunther was lying on his back with a huge boulder of a rock on top of him, so heavy he could hardly breathe. As Gunther cried and pleaded, he suddenly realized it was Alex and Lank.

"Please, I beg you to help me. I am going to die if you don't push this thing off me," Gunther gasped while he was short changed on air.

Lank looked at Alex and nodded slightly after a long pause. They stepped toward the rock and began to push with all their might. After what seemed like forever, they eventually moved the rock from Gunther. Gunther cried with shame, gratitude and disbelief. Lank reached out his hand to touch Gunther's stomach. His fluorescent yellow strength healed Gunther's entire body.

"Thank you, thank you. You've saved my life," Gunther wept.

Lank pulled Gunther up on to his feet and gave him the biggest hug he could muster. Alex joined in and hugged them both and they all began to cry together, so grateful to be alive.

"We have to find my mom, Tobi and Uncle Willy,"

Alex stated as she came back to her senses.

"This way," Gunther hollered with assertion. Gunther happened to have a compass in his pocket, the crafty hunter he was.

Gunther led the way through all the rubble and fallen trees. This earthquake was no joke, as almost everything in their sight was flattened and dismantled. Houses and cars were shattered. It was not a sight anyone should ever have to see. As they drew closer and closer in the direction of their place, nothing was recognizable.

"We just have to continue north," Gunther informed.

As they hobbled further with all kinds of bumps, scrapes and bruises, yet no broken bones, they came to a tree that was all too familiar to Alex.

"Look, Lank. There's the tree, where you left the ghost flower for me and the same spot I left you that note. The tree is still standing!" Alex exclaimed.

As they walked closer and closer to the tree, they realized that that was the only tree still standing. Alex looked to her left and realized her house was completely destroyed. Horrified, Alex turned her head back towards the tree. As she drew closer, she could see feet sticking out behind the tree.

"Mom! Willy! Is that you?" she hollered.

Sure enough, to her surprise, her mom and Willy's heads appeared, poking out to the side of the tree. Relieved and ecstatic, Alex ran towards her mom to give her a huge hug, the kind of hug that makes you never want to let go. Willy giggled as he hugged them both at the same time.

"Come here, Lank," Alex demanded.

Lank walked in for a group hug and by some miracle Willy and her mom weren't startled or scared as they embraced his arms around them, while Gunther sheepishly joined in.

Chapter 37

Lank's stomach was stabbing with hunger as he realized he hadn't eaten anything in days. Lank pointed to the top of the hill and Alex knew he was going to look for ghost flowers. As Lank reached the top and found the spot that had been covered in ghost flowers, all he could see were scattered ghost flowers amongst branches and trees that were completely mangled. The ghost flowers were crushed and hardly recognizable, mixed into the dirt as Lank took a closer look. Disappointed, Lank was about to head back down but stopped dead in his tracks, looked down and then slowly looked up. Lank signaled his hand to notify the group to come to where he was standing. As they drew near, climbing over all of the rubble, Lank pointed to the ground. When they all reached the hole, he was pointing at, it looked like a hole that led into complete darkness. They could see stars scattered across the black mass which seemed to lead to nowhere, the night's sky underground viewed through this tunnel; it appeared to be a deep starry black hole.

Alex looked down the starry black hole, dumbfounded. And just like that, she realized what was happening before her very eyes. She could see bubbles floating up towards the ground, and she could see Lank-like creatures inside of them. Immediately, she knew they were Lank's relatives, arriving to help restore planet Earth, because humans could no longer do it alone.

THE END

To read the Ghost Flower Legend, go to:
https://wsharing.com/WSphotosIndianPipe.htm

Manufactured by Amazon.ca
Bolton, ON

OCT 1 9 2021